GINGERBREAD INN

CHRISTMAS AT THE INN

BOOK 13

MAXINE DOUGLAS

The Christmas at the Inn Series

Pine Tree Inn by Nina Jayne
Cranberry Inn by Lynn A. Coleman
Fir Tree Inn by C.K. Johnson
Holly Bough Inn by Linda Carrol-Bradd
Merry Hallow Inn by Michele Pollock Dalton
Kissing Bough Inn by Lynn Crain
Starlight Inn by Anne Jones
Silver Bell Inn by J M Davies
Sugar Plum Inn by Lucinda Race
Apple Cider Inn, by Lorah Jaiyn
Snow Kissed Inn by Jessica Parker
Gingerbread Inn by Maxine Douglas
Snowflake Inn by Julie Castle
Evergreen Inn by London James
Reindeer Inn by Farrah Lee
Sleigh Bells Inn by Katie O'Connor
Holly Berry Inn by Nancy Fraser
Kris Kringle Inn by Joi Copeland
Sugar Cookie Inn by Kathryn LeBlanc
Winter Wonderland Inn by Merri Maywether
Miracle Inn by Regina Walker

ABOUT THE BOOK

Do you believe in second chances?
Neither did Nikki Reed nor Seth Jermaine until they found each
other wrapped in the magic of Christmas at the Gingerbread Inn.

Seth Jermaine's life is turned upside down when a long-lost love checks him into the Gingerbread Inn where they first met twenty years ago. They say absence makes the heart grow fonder, but Seth is knocked for a loop when someone from his past arrives and Nikki seems to lose all interest in rekindling their feelings.

A long ago romantic who gave up on love, Nikki Reed starts to look at life differently when an old crush checks into the Gingerbread Inn for a winter wedding. Drawn to each other, Nikki becomes unsure of Seth's faithfulness when the past starts popping up and other commitments distract Seth causing her to wonder if their rekindled relationship is only history repeating itself.

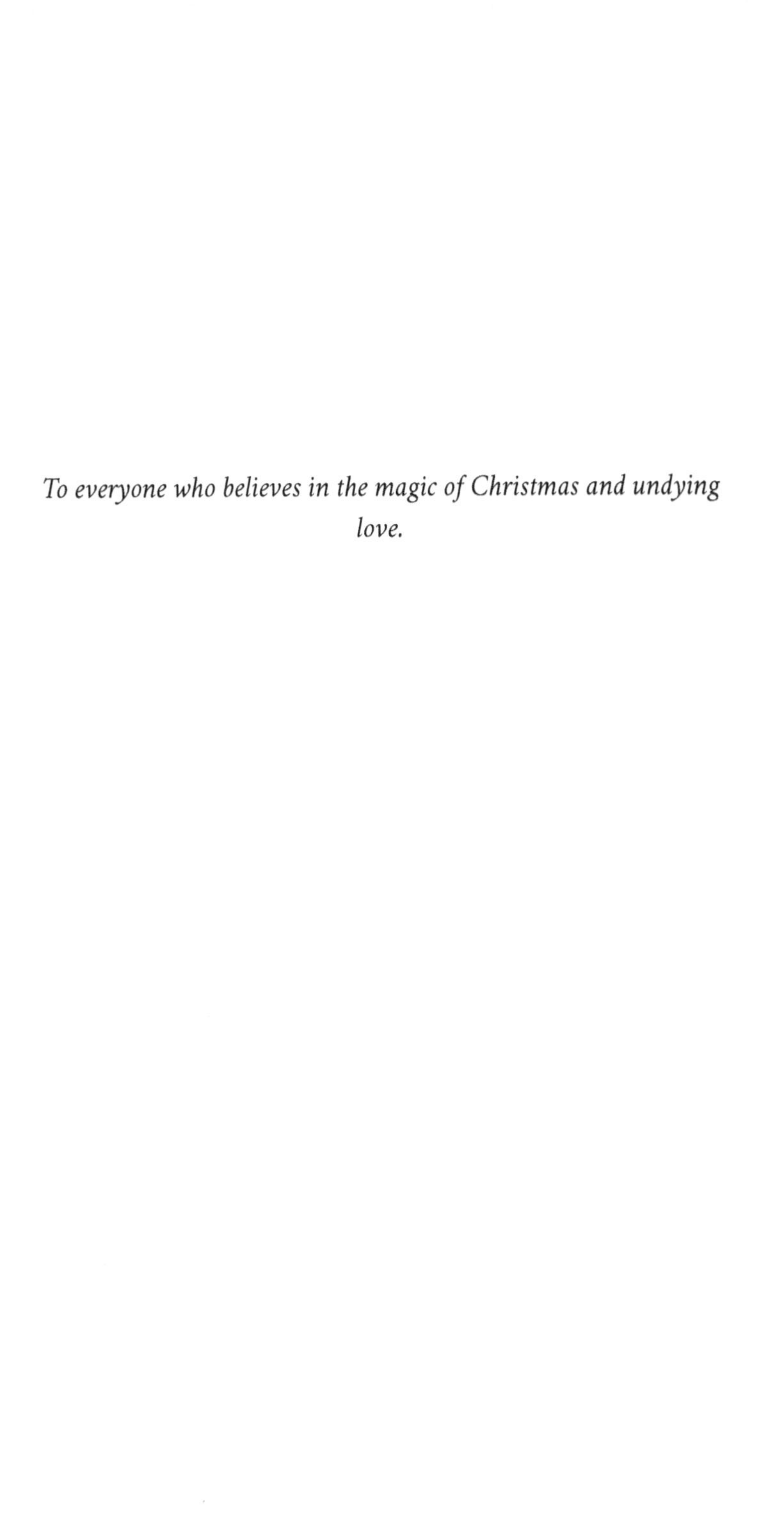

To everyone who believes in the magic of Christmas and undying love.

ACKNOWLEDGMENTS

Recipes are inspired from *The Passionate Palate* by Desiree Witkowski, D.T.R.

CHAPTER ONE

The snow-capped mountains shimmered in the morning sun. If one looked close enough, tiny snowflakes promised more snow. Jack Frost had painted several masterpieces on the inn's floor-to-ceiling oak-framed lobby windows.

Nicole Reed, Nikki to those who knew her well, took a deep breath as the warm aroma of cinnamon, nutmeg and ginger edged with the sweetness of molasses and honey filled her senses with comfort and joy.

Gingerbread. One of the reasons she fell in love with the inn. One, but not the one that played havoc with her emotions for the past thirty years.

The Gingerbread Inn had become home to her long after college, following years of floating from one job to another in the hospitality field, and the tragedy which upended her seemingly ideal life. Several years after her husband Tony died, Nikki finally decided to use the life insurance money to buy the fledging inn. It had been the place where her heart was first broken; now it was a place which gave her peace.

Loud voices and shouting slammed into her serene mood like a blast of freezing cold from Canada. *Now what?* she thought, slipping into boss mode as she headed in the direction of the chaos. *I can only guess what this is all about.*

"Would someone mind telling me what the shouting is for? In case you've all forgotten, there are rooms to prepare for the guests that will begin to arrive," Nikki said, stepping through the kitchen's swinging doors as her chef stood at the counter packing up his knives.

"I will not share *my* kitchen and *my* staff with another chef," Chef Miles Winston shouted, his eyes blazing in jealous anger.

Nikki looked at Miles, assessing the situation quickly. This wasn't the first time he'd thrown a temper tantrum. Yes, Chef Winston was a bit of a prima donna. Yes, he could be difficult to work with at times. But he was an award-winning chef with a vast knowledge of gingerbread recipes, the main reason she'd hired him in the first place.

"Chef, is that what you're upset about? Sharing the inn's kitchen and your staff with a chef that the wedding planner hired at the request of the bride's family?" Nikki asked, moving slowly toward Miles. "The entire inn has been reserved for this wedding. There will be no other guests checking in until after the new year. So, in reality, this is a great opportunity for you to take a paid vacation."

"Vacation? Why would I take a vacation?" Miles asked, staring at her with a mixture of shock and resentment in his eyes. "I've never taken a vacation in my forty years as a chef."

"Because, Chef, you haven't had one for, as you said, in forty years and you, if for no other reason, deserves to go home for the holidays," Nikki pointed out gently.

"And when I return? What then?" Miles asked. "Will I find I've been replaced? That this kitchen is no longer a place of welcome?"

"The kitchen will be as it was when you left," Nikki promised. "You will always have a place here for as long you like. You are much needed and respected by everyone, especially by me."

"And my sous-chef and staff?" Miles asked, waving an arm through the air.

"We will all be here as well, Chef." A chorus of voices sang out from every corner of the kitchen.

"We will not desert you, Chef," his sous-chef Gabby promised from the pantry doorway.

"See, nothing to worry about at all," Nikki confirmed, placing a hand on Miles's shoulder "Now, I expect the wedding planner and her staff to be arriving in a few days. Our last guest checked out yesterday, so you can make your travel plans today.

"I'm sure there are enough supplies in the pantry to get us through the next week or two. And you've trained your staff so well that none of us will go hungry in your absence."

"Yes, Ms. Reed, as you suggest." Miles reluctantly conceded surrendering his staff to the unknown chef. "I will let my family know to expect me for Christmas."

"Thank you, Chef." Nikki smiled, leaving the kitchen with a sense of accomplishment she'd put out a rather large fire.

Strolling into the inn's restaurant, Nikki paused near the

overly large windows with a beautiful view of Christmas Mountain. The tiny snowflakes had blossomed into large fluffy cotton balls, the kind that are great to catch on the tip of the tongue. A giggle escaped from the little girl deep inside her.

She closed her eyes. Memories floated through her mind like the preview of a movie. A movie about a time of innocence when she believed all things were possible at the inn on Christmas Mountain.

"Ms. Reed," Ashley, the inn's very capable and perky desk clerk, called out.

"Yes, Ashley what is it?" Nikki asked, quickly swiping away the lone tear staining one cheek, then turning around.

"Thomas received a call from the airport. He is on his way to pick up the chef for next week's wedding," Ashley answered.

"Thank you," Nikki said, taking a cleansing breath to clear her head. "A few days early, isn't he?"

"I would say so," Ashley answered, spinning around to return to her duties at the very quiet front desk.

"Let's hope his and Miles's paths don't cross. I've told Miles to take a vacation and was hoping he'd have been gone before this chef arrived," Nikki muttered, following Ashley into the lobby, then crossing the white tiled floor to her office. "Looks like I may have another fire to put out."

* * *

THE SMALL AIRPORT bustled with passengers of every age group. Families with young children. Couples. Singles traveling either alone or with a tour group over the holiday break. Some carried skis on their shoulders. Others grabbed bags as the conveyor belt continued to circle. On the other side of the pane of windows, falling snow gathered on the surface here and there.

Seth Jermaine stood by the door waiting for the driver from the Gingerbread Inn to arrive. Part of him looked forward to returning to the inn on Christmas Mountain, while another part felt the sadness of his youth so long ago.

The last time he'd arrived at Christmas Mountain Village, he'd been with his college buddies ready to take the slopes. And anything, or anyone, that crossed their line of vision. The one thing he hadn't been prepared for was losing his heart to a pretty little blonde with eyes the color of a clear blue summer sky and just as warm.

After a week-long whirlwind romance, he'd wanted nothing more than to go home, break off his engagement, and come back before the girl who stole his heart vanished.

But fate had other plans. Plans that didn't bring him back to the Gingerbread Inn until now. Back to slay the dragons of a young man's fanciful hopes and dreams.

"Seth Jermaine. Paging Seth Jermaine to the nearest courtesy phone."

Hearing his name blast over the intercom, Seth grabbed his bags and headed for the nearest airport courtesy phone. "Seth Jermaine," he said into the receiver.

"Mr. Jermaine, the car is here for the Gingerbread Inn. Please proceed to the pickup area."

"Thank you," he said, hanging up the phone. Bags slung over his shoulder, Seth wove his way through the crowd until he reached the pickup area where his car waited for him.

"Mr. Jermaine?" the man waiting at the open trunk of the car asked as Seth handed over his bags.

"Yes," he replied then slid into the backseat. The driver closed Seth's door, sat behind the wheel, and drove away from the airport as smooth as an ice skater on ice.

The falling snow continued to shimmer off the passing landscape. The driver maneuvered the car skillfully up the mountain road leading to the inn. Seth had forgotten how beautiful it was here. Unless memory failed him, not much had changed in thirty years.

"Has any of the wedding party started to arrive?" Seth asked, hoping he'd have a few days to himself to get the lay of the land.

"No, sir. You are the first," the driver answered. "If you need to leave the inn at any time, please call down to the desk and ask them to tell me when and where you wish to go."

"And your name?" Seth asked, catching the driver's glance in the rearview mirror.

"Thomas, sir," Thomas said, averting his eyes back to the road.

"Thank you, Thomas. I will do that if I need to." Seth leaned his head against the backseat.

"Very well, sir," Thomas replied.

The twenty-minute ride seemed to pass quickly. Before he knew it, they'd pulled up in front of the inn. Seth heard the trunk pop open moments after his door swung open.

"Welcome to the Gingerbread Inn, sir," Thomas said, walking ahead of him with Seth's bags in his hands.

Seth didn't realize he'd been holding his breath until he walked through the doors. The fresh scent of pine was replaced by the spicey aroma of gingerbread. His gaze swept across the lobby. The once large woodsy furniture his mind's eye remembered had been replaced by country modern furniture placed sparsely around the room.

"Looks like I may have another fire to put out."

Seth watched the blonde woman scurry across the lobby and into an office, the door closing behind her. *It can't be*, he thought, cocking his head as a memory sprung forward. An all too familiar one at that.

"No, not possible," he muttered.

"Are you ready to check in, Chef…" the girl behind the desk asked.

"Jermaine, Seth Jermaine," Seth answered, still wondering if he'd been dreaming. He had to be. After thirty years there was no possible way Nichole would be here now.

"Seth?"

Seth turned slowly. The woman who'd just gone into the office stood several feet in front of him. Her blue eyes were wide with questions and something he couldn't quite describe.

"Nikki Dutcher?" he asked, his heart slamming against his chest.

"It's Nichole Reed now," Nikki answered finding her breath again, wondering if she'd been dropped into an alternate world. "You're the chef?"

"Yes, I am. I didn't know…" Seth stammered, taking a few steps closer to her.

"Great!" Nikki exclaimed a bit too cheerfully, trembling

inside and out. Every ounce of her responded to him as if thirty years hadn't passed. "Since you've only just arrived, take time to settle in and I'll have someone show you the kitchen tomorrow."

"I would much rather see the kitchen right away," Seth said giving her that crooked smile that made her feel special. "The sooner I inspect the pantry, refrigerator and freezer, the sooner I will know what I need to order."

"As you wish," Nikki said wishing she'd never come out of her office. "Ashley, please have Gabby come out and show Chef Jermaine the kitchen."

"Thank you, Nikki," Seth said.

"Ms. Reed, Chef Jermaine," Nikki responded holding her head up high. "I keep a professional relationship with my employees."

"*Your* employees?"

"Yes. I have owned the Gingerbread Inn for a few years. I am sure you will find everything in order. Chef Winston is very particular about *his* kitchen," Nikki said loving the look of surprise on his face.

"Well, it's a good thing I'm not one of *your* employees then," Seth replied closing the distance between them.

"You do have a point there." Nikki sidestepped Seth's uncomfortable advance. "However, it is the inn's kitchen and there are protocols to be followed."

"I thought you said it was your chef's kitchen." Seth grinned sending an annoying message she'd almost forgotten.

"They are one and the same, Chef Jermaine." Nikki clucked, mentally kicking herself for losing her composure.

"So this person is the reason for my unplanned vacation," Miles spat coming down the log stairway with a well-worn suitcase.

"Chef Jermaine is only here for the wedding, as you well know, Chef," Nikki replied as the two men eyed each other up. "Chef Winston meet Chef Jermaine."

There may have been several inches difference in height, but Miles stood toe-to-toe with Seth. Nikki had no idea how Seth matched up to Miles as a chef, but she did know Miles wasn't going to let the taller and younger Seth think he was a pushover.

"What is your specialty, Chef?" Miles asked, his five-foot seven-inch height seemingly matching Seth's six feet.

"I specialize in making my clients happy," Seth responded his gaze hard on the older chef.

"Excellent, then as Ms. Reed has assured me, you are *not* my replacement." Miles turned away, a slight spring in his step as he walked out the door to where the inn's car waited for him.

"I've heard of Winston. Is he always like that?" Seth asked.

"As a matter-of-fact that was mild. Chef Winston is an expert when it comes to gingerbread," Nikki replied pride filling her to the brim. She'd worked hard to secure Miles and she wasn't about to let him go until he was ready to retire.

"So all he knows is gingerbread? Must be boring for your guests," Seth jabbed.

"Maybe you need to brush up on your *James Beard* chefs. You'll find Chef Winston among the most sought-after chefs who decided a quieter life was more suitable for him," Nikki informed, her gaze on movement in the dining room.

"Gabby, this is Chef Jermaine. Please give him a tour of the kitchen, pantry and refrigerator. Also order whatever supplies the chief needs while he is here for the Hathaway wedding.

"Chef Jermaine, I'm positive you'll find the kitchen staff willing to please you and follow your instructions to the tee. Enjoy your stay with us," Nikki said then turned and went back to her office where she could regroup. She needed to figure out how to handle the unexpected appearance of the ghost of past heartache.

CHAPTER TWO

*S*eth was pretty sure he'd have to make a second trip to inspect the pantry to make sure he hadn't missed anything. Gabby led him through the kitchen but he couldn't concentrate on sugar, spices, vegetables and other such things. He wanted to talk to Nikki to catch up and see if they could be friends. To explain what happened thirty years ago.

Leaving the kitchen with a list of items he'd need for the upcoming wedding, he strolled through the restaurant pausing in front of the windows overlooking the slopes.

"Who would have guessed after all these years Nikki Dutcher would be here," Seth muttered watching snow come down a bit heavier than it had been an hour ago. The slopes were going to be great for skiing if the wedding party didn't get snowed in at the airport.

"She had said her last name was Reed; where is her husband? What about children, does she have any?" Thankfully he and Payton never did, one of the many reasons for their split.

The more he tried to work through the possible answers the more questions arose. He wanted to know every nuance of her life. If she had married, she'd obviously gotten over him all those years ago. Or had she settled just as he had?

"I never tire of this scene." Nikki's voice floated softly to him. "Even in the spring, summer, and fall the mountains are beautiful, only in different ways."

"The winters are—" Seth turned around, his gaze admiring her beautiful face, "magical."

"Yes, you could put it that way." Nikki stood a few feet from him, her jasmine scent filling his senses with memories.

"Nikki, I—" Seth began, unable to voice the thoughts in his mind. How could he when he struggled against the temptation to take her in his arms?

"Did you find the kitchen adequate, Chef?" Nikki asked, averting her gaze from him.

"Yes, I have made a list of items I'll need. I'm afraid it is quite lengthy," Seth said, feeling oddly uncomfortable. He'd never felt this way with anyone before, not even total strangers.

"And the kitchen staff, will you be able to work with them as well?" Nikki asked, staring out the window.

"I don't see a problem with the staff, the layout of the kitchen, or anything else you might be concerned about," Seth said waving his arms in the air. "What is it you are really asking me, Nikki?"

She turned. Tears glistened in her blue eyes like flakes of snow in the sun. "Whether or not you can be professional while here given our ancient history." Nikki held her head high despite the small quivering in her chin. "Did you take this job because you knew I would be here?"

"In case you couldn't tell, I am as surprised as you are." Seth shook his head. "Was I that hard to read earlier?"

"Last time I thought I could read you I was totally wrong. Believe me, I'll not make that mistake again," Nikki whispered, her hands pressed against the pane of glass. "Fool me once…"

"You've got to let me try to explain, Nikki," Seth said quietly, taking her hand in his. "If nothing else, I hope we can be friends. If not for always, at least while I'm here."

"Explain what? Why you broke my heart? Or why you never called me like you promised you would?" Nikki pulled her hand from his and folded her arms around herself. "And it's Nicole. Ms. Reed when my employees are present."

"All right then, Nicole. I didn't mean to hurt you. I went home to break things off, but lost my nerve," Seth admitted feeling like a twenty-something idiot with no brain cells again. "I never forgot you, or that Christmas vacation."

"That was a lifetime ago, Seth," Nikki whispered. "I'm not sure I want to revisit it."

"At least have dinner with me before everyone else arrives or we won't have a moment alone," Seth asked hoping against the odds that she'd agree.

NIKKI STIFLED the urge to say "yes" too quickly. Even though she wanted to know everything he'd done for the past thirty years, she didn't want to appear too eager.

She'd noticed the shadow of a band on his left ring

finger telling her he'd been married. She wondered what happened. Was he a widower? Or one of the many casualties of a broken marriage?

She hoped it was the latter. She knew all too well what grieving a dead spouse felt like. It was the worst ordeal she'd ever had to experience; one she never wanted none too soon to repeat, if ever again.

At least a divorce left you guilt-free to get on with your life. To meet someone to date; maybe even establish a long-term relationship that could lead to something that had been missing the first time around.

Did Seth have children or grandchildren?

What had made him decide to become a chef when he'd been going to college for engineering?

Did he still live in Oklahoma? Or had he moved to New York City or Las Vegas where all the high-profile chefs had well-known restaurants?

So many unanswered questions. Only one way to find out the answers. Agree to have dinner with him. One dinner and nothing more.

"Nicole, will you please have dinner with me?" Seth asked again, a thread of hope in his question.

"Against my better judgement, yes, I'll have dinner with you," Nikki agreed feeling the cloud that hung over her since Tony's death dissipate slightly.

"Great!" Seth grinned. "Meet me here in a few hours, then."

"I need a specific time, Seth. My people depend on me and I'm not going to let them down," Nikki said mentally running through the rest of her day's calendar. "I'll meet you at five."

"Five it is. Good thing I'm a chef," Seth teased then turned back toward the kitchen.

A mixed bag of emotions spilled over Nikki. She wasn't that twenty-something girl who didn't really understand how things worked. She'd learned that lesson long ago.

"I'm not falling for it again," Nikki muttered making her way back to her office. "No matter what charming antic he pulls that worked before. They are *not* going to work again."

Closing the office door behind her, she stood at the window overlooking nature's bounty. New snow always made her feel it was a fresh beginning.

Was that what Seth being here was? A fresh start?

Could they finish what had not ended so well years go? Or was she hoping they could have a fresh start and continue where they'd left off?

What was she thinking? That a thirty-year-old wound scabbed over should be picked open and allowed to fester again?

Because somewhere in her heart there was a place of hope. Hope for what had once been to be again.

SETH RUMMAGED through the pantry and refrigerator. He'd sent the kitchen staff on their way telling them to report first thing in the morning. He had to prepare this meal on his own.

He was surprised at how easily remembering Nikki's favorite things to eat came. She loved breakfast for supper. She also loved carnival food. How to combine them was the question.

He could make funnel cakes using a sweet apple pancake

mix. Top them off with a berry sauce and whipped cream. And to drink a root beer float followed by Swiss coffee.

Feeling confident, he found all the ingredients. Setting up the *misen en place* for the dry ingredients, Seth started peeling and cutting the apples. Setting them aside, he started on the berries.

His heart pounding, Seth glanced down at his watch. "Where did the time go?" he muttered placing a heavy skillet on the stove, adding vegetable oil, and turning the stove on medium heat. He combined all his ingredients while the oil heated to 350°F.

He had less than an hour to get everything perfect and give Nikki something special. Something that would bring back happy memories. Things to let her know he remembered everything about her.

Pouring the pancake mixture into a piping bag, Seth squeezed the batter in a circular motion into the oil until a large disk formed. He repeated the process until he had several funnel cakes set aside in the warmer.

The fragrance of the apples and oatmeal made the kitchen smell like Christmas morning. Visions of his mother cooking and baking filled his mind and heart with happiness. He missed those holidays when the family gathered; all that stopped after his parents moved into a small apartment and started traveling more after his dad retired.

"Dang it!" he muttered under his breath glancing at the clock on the wall. "No time to lose."

He trotted over to the cabinet and pulled two to-go-boxes down from a shelf. Placing a funnel cake in each one, he spread the fresh berry sauce over them then topped each with fresh whipped cream. The ice cream was already in mugs in the freezer so all he had to do was pour root beer into the glasses. The Swiss coffee was ready as well.

Placing everything onto a large serving tray, Seth walked into the dining room and over to a table at one of the windows. Within a matter of moments, he had everything on the table then ran back into the kitchen to deposit the tray. Grabbing the cups of Swiss coffee, he reached the table as Nikki walked into the dining room.

"Why does it smell like I'm at the fair?" she asked sounding like a kid.

"Have a seat," he said, pulling out a chair for her. "I wanted this to be special and not so formal. I hope I haven't totally blown it for you."

"Well to-go-boxes are a bit of a surprise." Sitting down, Nikki folded her napkin across her lap. "And I haven't had a good root beer float in some time."

"I hope it lives up to your expectations," he said taking the seat across from her.

Reaching across the table, he was pleased when she covered his hand with hers.

"Come, Lord Jesus, be our Guest, and let these gifts to us be blessed. Amen," they prayed in unison.

"These to-go-boxes have me intrigued," she said lifting it to her nose and sniffing. "Oh my, whatever is in here smells like I'm at the fair."

The smile on her face gave him confidence that he'd done the right thing in bringing something different to the table.

"May I?" she asked, setting the container down.

"Of course, dig in!" he said watching her. He wanted to

see the expression on her face the moment she opened the box.

"A funnel cake!" she exclaimed her eyes twinkling.

"Yes, with a twist. I used my favorite pancake mix, so you can have breakfast for supper," Seth explained feeling a bit prideful.

"You remembered," Nikki responded her eyes glistening.

"There are a lot of things I remember, Nikki," Seth said softly, his gaze locked onto hers.

Nikki blinked then dug into the funnel cake, slowly slipping a piece into her mouth. "Mmmm, this is divine, Seth. I could eat this every day if I wouldn't gain a pound."

"I thought it would be nice to have a bit of Christmas before the craziness happened. Once the wedding party arrives I'm not sure how much time I'll have for quiet moments like this," Seth said, opening his box and slicing into the sweet breakfast treat inside.

"It is nice and thank you for remembering," Nikki said softly smiling as she sipped the root beer float through the red and white striped straw.

"You're welcome," Seth replied watching her between bites.

They sat in comfortable silence through dinner until it was time to sit back and enjoy the Swiss coffee.

"Tell me what you've been doing since we last..." Seth began.

"Saw each other?" Nikki finished.

"Yes, if you are willing to tell an old friend," Seth said, watching her expression change. It was going to take some time for her to trust him again, that much he knew.

"Friend?" Nikki asked her brows furrowed. "Are we really friends, Seth?"

"I would like to think that we could be once again," Seth said, each word containing hope and encouragement.

"I'm not sure I'm ready to revisit that friendship," Nikki said, pushing away from the table. "Thank you for dinner. It was a really nice surprise and tasted wonderful. I really must be getting back to work for, as you indicated, there is a wedding party due to arrive and I must make sure everything is ready. Good night, Seth."

"Wait," Seth called out to no avail as Nikki walked out of the dining room stomping on his heart with each footfall.

CHAPTER THREE

"Hold all my calls, Ashley," Nikki instructed as she quickly passed by the front desk.

"Of course, Ms. Reed," Ashley answered looking up from behind the counter.

Nikki strolled past her closed office door, down the hall until she reached her personal living quarters. Unlocking the door with a key card, she pushed open the door and took a deep breath.

The two guest rooms converted into one living space was the perfect size for her year around. It was her home where the outside world couldn't squeeze its tentacles around her.

If any of her staff needed to reach her, they'd use text messaging. In her opinion it was a phone function which destroyed any form of verbal conversation between two or more people. She despised it more than anything else.

More than Seth Jermaine? Maybe.

To be fair, they might be on equal ground except her feelings toward Seth were deeper and longer. So much so she didn't feel ready to become *friends* on any level with him.

"What business is it of his what my life has been like? He doesn't need to know what I've been doing!" Nikki shuffled around her small open concept living room and kitchen straightening things that didn't need it.

"Did he truly believe we could be *friends* after what he did to me?" Opening the dishwasher, she put away the few items left from the last time she'd run it. "He's asking too much without an explanation as to why he broke his promise."

Nikki stood in the middle of her small galley kitchen with every cupboard door opened. The last time she'd been like this was when she'd been mourning her husband after the car accident that took his life.

Mourning wasn't the right word as she still mourned Tony. Angry was more like it. Furious might be a better description of the way she'd been feeling. Tony's death had felt like a betrayal. A betrayal to their love and the promise of growing old together. A forever that didn't happen.

Now for the third time in her life those same feelings surfaced again. The unspoken emotion of deception by the two men in her life she'd given her heart to. The only difference being the first was alive and staying in her little inn.

With the audacity of looking just as handsome as the day he walked away; albeit a bit older and grayer around the temples but still holding that youthfulness.

One-by-one, Nikki closed each cupboard door with a soft puff. Lifting a coffee cup off a shelf, she closed the last door as quietly as the others.

"Sure wish I had grabbed that Swiss coffee on the way

out," she murmured settling for the K-cup she popped into the coffee maker. It was a new flavor she still wasn't quite sure she cared for.

Calming down as the coffee brewed, Nikki realized she'd acted like an unhinged girl. Seth didn't deserve to be treat like that. He was a guest in her inn and he should be shown the same respect as any other guest would receive.

Instead, she'd walked away spewing nonsense at him. She'd disrespected him and she wasn't proud of it.

"I'll apologize first thing in the morning," she promised removing the cup from under the last drip of steaming coffee.

SETH STOOD outside Nikki's door with what he hoped was a peace offering in his hand.

After she had stormed out of the dining room, he'd felt like a whipped dog. The sweet young lady he once knew had turned into a woman who wasn't afraid to speak her mind and didn't mince words. Even though her message was loud and clear, he wasn't about to run away. Not again.

As he'd cleared away what was left of their disastrous meal, he'd noticed she hadn't drank the Swiss coffee which was one of her biggest cravings thirty years ago. Once he'd gotten everything cleaned up in the kitchen, he set about making a fresh batch and walked through the inn until he found the door labeled *Private.* He stood there and resisted the temptation to press his ear against it, let alone knock.

So why did he hesitate? What's the worst she could do? Open the door, take the tray, say thank you, then unceremoniously close it? Or simply open and close the door on him without a single word?

No matter which scenario played out, they had to settle things between them or the next several days were going to be uncomfortable. Not only for the two of them, but also for the staff and the wedding party due to arrive by week's end.

"Here goes," he muttered then knocked on the door. "Nikki?"

"Go away, Seth, I'm busy," she called out her voice muffled by the door between them.

"Come on, Nikki. I come in peace," Seth answered. "I brought Swiss coffee with me."

The lock clicked and the door opened. She stood before him looking as unsettled as he felt.

"Come on in," she said opening the door for him to walk through with the tray. "Just put the tray on the counter and then leave, please."

"Nikki, I'm not running away this time." Seth set everything down and stood his ground. He wasn't going to let her run him off until they at least tried to settled things between them.

"I'll call down to the front desk then."

"No, you won't," he remarked carrying two cups over to the overstuffed chairs and a side table.

"You're right, I won't but sure would like to. What is it you want now, Seth?"

"Like it or not, we need to talk to each other in a civil manner. The way I figure it if we don't, this wedding may end up being a disaster and so will the inn's reputation."

Seth waited for her to cross the room and sit down before he sat.

"I don't know what you expect from me," Nikki said sitting softly in the chair.

"How about a chance to explain what happened back then." Seth sat on the edge of his chair. He didn't want her to think he wasn't taking this seriously.

Nothing was more important to him than letting Nikki know why he never contacted her again.

"I KNOW WHAT HAPPENED, Seth. You left without a memory of us and what we shared that Christmas." The words sounded as sorrowful as the way she felt. Yet, if he hadn't abandoned her, she never would have met and been loved by Tony. And she wouldn't change that even if she could. "Truth be told, you did me a favor and I have no regrets for the way my life has been."

"I'm happy for you, Nikki but you're wrong in thinking I forgot about you. While something was happening between you and I, something else was happening back home I didn't have the power to stop," Seth sat back in the chair looking like a defeated man.

What had happened to that young man of the modern ages? The man who oozed confidence thirty years ago was gone—at least for the moment.

"You expect me to believe that? The only thing that could have stopped you coming back was a commitment to another woman."

And there it was. The look on his face. The affirmation

that she'd spoken the words before he could. There had been someone else before they'd met.

She shouldn't be surprised. He was good looking, intelligent, and well-liked by everyone that Christmas. Why would she think things were any different for him at home?

"Engagements are broken all the time, Seth. Unless…" *No! It couldn't be that there had been a baby to be considered. Or at least the chance of a baby.* "Was she…"

"Pregnant? No, nothing like that." Seth affirmed, a faint glint of sadness in his eyes.

The wave of relief that soared through her quickly crashed and burned. If not the possibility of a baby, then what?

"Although it may have been easier if Payton had been pregnant compared to what had happened," Seth muttered, running his hands through his hair.

"Go ahead, I'm listening. But I can't promise you it'll change anything." Nikki was now more curious than she'd have thought she would be to know why someone had broken her young heart the way Seth had. Still, she wasn't sure anything he had to say would change her feelings toward him.

"I had every intention of honoring my promise to you. You had my heart completely. You were all I ever thought about for years until all hope disappeared from my mind." Seth shoved out of the chair and walked over to the window overlooking one of the ski sloops. "If nothing else, I hope you'll see that my honor is my weakest strength."

Nikki watched him push the curtain aside and stare out the window. She saw his anxiety when he glanced at her. The hurt surfacing from its depths took her by surprise.

"When I got home, I told my parents of my intentions. To finish school and marry a girl I fell head over heels with. You can imagine their reaction. Their son telling them all their hard work to get him connected with the *right* family was all for nothing.

"The Sinclairs were from *old* New York and Mr. Sinclair had been my father's business partner for over twenty years. But our families go back much further than those twenty years. At one time even though the Sinclairs and the Jermaines were financially equals, we were what they called *new* money."

"Are you talking back to the time of the gilded age?" Nikki asked astonished those rules still existed today. "I thought that kind of thinking died out long ago."

"Yes, well, there were rules to be followed then as there is now. Rules that I stopped following after Payton and I split up years ago," Seth mumbled under this breath.

"So you are separated? Or divorced?" Nikki's heart pounded, waiting for his answer. Was he truly free after all these years?

And why in the world should she care or even be interested in his current marital status, or lack thereof?

"Divorced soon after Payton realized that I was not going to follow in my father's footsteps and pick up the reins of Jermaine Industries after all. But I'm getting ahead of myself and that doesn't explain why I didn't come back for you."

"No it doesn't, and I'm not sure I want to hear it since you are obviously out of my financial realm. My family is anything but *old* or *new* money." Nikki held her head high. She was proud of the kind of stock that made up her DNA.

She came from one hundred percent hard working, blue collar for generations.

"Yes, I know. I know exactly where your family comes from. Good, honest, hard-working people who cared less about money and more about honor and family." Seth looked at her, his soft expression turning hard. "My father made sure I knew that when I got home that Christmas."

"He, he knew about my family? But how?" Nikki gasped. "And why am I not surprised after what you've told me so far?"

"That Christmas, I'd forgotten about his network of spies that followed me everywhere I went. I'd never given them much thought because they'd always been there my entire life," Seth sat back down, close enough she could almost hear his heart beating.

"They knew everything and reported back to your father?" Nikki asked.

"Like I said, when I got home and told my father of my plans he told me of his. If I didn't marry Payton Sinclair as planned, he was going to make sure your family was destroyed both financially and socially.

"I had to protect you, Nikki. I had to marry Payton to protect you and your family."

CHAPTER FOUR

The sudden stillness in the room felt like skiing down the slopes with no end in sight and a monster of a blizzard on the horizon.

Cold.

Silent.

Deadly.

"Please say something, Nikki," Seth pleaded reaching out to take her hand only to have her snatch it away.

"You expect me to believe that your father would stoop so low to keep you from marrying the 'wrong sort' of girl?" Nikki looked at him with a mixture of disbelief and astonishment in her eyes. "My father is very capable of taking care of himself and his family, no matter who tries to do whatever to him. Everyone knows him to be honest and trustworthy."

"I know it's hard to believe, Nikki. I saw the file folder on your father with my own eyes. When they couldn't find anything incriminating against him, my father fabricated a story that was signed by several witnesses." Seth sat back in the chair afraid that if he didn't keep the distance between them he'd reach out for her again. He knew if he did she'd run from him, and he didn't want that. Not if there was a slight possibility of being reunited.

"He threatened to carry out his plan if I didn't follow through and marry Payton. And I knew my father well enough to know he would do whatever he had to in order to get what he wanted." Seth said unsure how much he should tell her. The trumped-up allegations on her father would most likely crush, then anger her beyond reason.

If she asked he'd have no choice but to tell her, but only after he tried to convince her it didn't matter anymore. That lies were better left unheard.

"But to ruin another man's life," Nikki began tears glistening in her eyes, "all because of me doesn't make sense."

"One must understand the history between the Sinclairs and the Jermaines. They have always been a ruthless bunch. Stomping down anyone who got in their way. I suspect it was how they managed to keep their wealth from one generation to another," Seth said avoiding making eye contact with her. "Until that day when a file folder with your name on it was tossed across the desk to me, I was proud of who I was. I was proud to carry the name of Jermaine.

"When I read the contents of that folder, I knew I had no choice in the matter. So that day I agreed to marry Payton Sinclair. I agreed to never make contact with you or my father's lawyers would carry out their orders. It was also the day I realized my life had never been my own and began exploring how to distance myself from my father and his shadiness. It took me years to find a way to cut those ties."

"That's why you gave up engineering and went to culinary school instead?" Nikki asked. The bitterness in her voice slightly softening gave him hope.

"Yes, but it took a few years for me to be able to put it all together. I had to make my father believe that I was going to take over the business when he retired. Payton believed with the combination of our families' wealth, she could do as she liked when she liked—and she did." Seth glanced over at Nikki surprised by the veil of sadness surfacing in her eyes.

"When there weren't any children coming forth, father pulled out that folder once again to remind me of what he could do."

"Your marriage was never—consummated?"

"I didn't say that. I made sure I always wore protection convincing Payton that the time wasn't right financially if we were going to give our children everything they needed and deserved. She didn't argue seeing it as a way to have more for herself." Seth knew it was a deception, but he knew his then wife well enough to know how to play to her vanity.

"But Father wasn't to be dissuaded from having an heir. He put his plan into play and went after your father to prove a point. It was then that I decided to have nothing to do with my father. I told Payton that I was going back to school to become a chef. She wasn't pleased."

"I remember an incident shortly after Tony and I were married. My parents fought for weeks about something Father continuously denied. Then one day, it was as if their fighting never happened," Nikki said her brows furrowing. "That was because of your father?"

"I'm ashamed to admit it was, but—" Seth began his heart racing, --you should know he may have started it and had nothing to do with ending it."

"I think you should leave," Nikki said, pushing out of the chair.

"But Nikki, you haven't heard—"

"I've heard quite enough, Seth Jermaine. You need to leave NOW," Nikki hissed holding the door open, her gaze cold and dark.

"We'll talk tomorrow after you've had time to think about what I've told you," Seth said standing in the hall wanting to chance away the pain of betrayal in her eyes.

"ONLY BECAUSE WE MUST. After this wedding is over, I don't know." Nikki quietly closed the door, leaving Seth standing alone in the hallway. Successfully shutting him out for the time being.

"One…two…three.." Nikki leaned against the door. Her heart pounding she closed her eyes and continued counting. "Four…five…six."

"Good night, Nikki."

Hearing his muffled voice, she pushed away from the door. Her heartbeat evened out for the first time since she'd let Seth into her apartment.

She felt betrayed by her sense of common courtesy. Given her position of owning the inn, she would have been hard pressed to continue her rudeness toward Seth. Not to mention her mother would have suggested some unpleasant chore for her to perform and think about the consequence of her actions.

"Eight o'clock," she noted looking at her watch. "Mom will have just finished watching her favorite show by now."

Nikki strolled across the room. Picking up the phone, she quickly dialed her parents' number and waited for the call to go through. Being in the mountains, she'd had landlines installed in the inn as cell reception was spotty at best.

"Nikki is everything okay?" her mom, Elaine Dutcher, asked after only two rings.

"Yes, all is well," Nikki answered plopping down in a chair before her legs gave out on her. She hadn't realized just how nervous she was until she'd heard her mother's voice.

"So why are you calling so late?" her mother's words were full of concern for her only child.

"It's not that late, Mom. And I know your show just ended," Nikki teased gathering her courage to possibly opening an old wound. "You'll never guess who checked into the inn for the wedding that reserved the inn for the rest of the month."

"Nicole don't play around with me. Just spit it out!" her mother said in that tone only mothers knew how to use. The one that children knew meant not to push their mother beyond her limits.

"Seth Jermaine." Nikki's heart sank hearing the gasp from her mother. "Mom?"

"What is he doing there?" her mother muttered.

"He's the chef for the wedding party I told you about, but that's not why I'm calling." Nikki leaned back in the chair wondering what she'd done to deserve Seth coming back into her life, even if for only a week.

"No, I imagine it's not," Elaine said.

"He told me an incredible story I find hard to believe." Nikki was always amazed at her mom. It was as if she had a sixth sense about things. About what Nikki needed to hear, or not hear. "I want to ask you if—"

"You want to know if he played a part in those ugly accusations made against your father thirty years ago. Am I right?

"What did he tell you?" Elaine asked quietly before continuing in a stronger voice. "Did he tell you his father trumped up a tale of infidelity that almost split us up if not for Seth's intervention?"

"So it's true then?" Nikki asked unable to define the feelings swirling in her. "He didn't say what the supposed evidence was, only that it was false. Now I understand why you both fought so much back then."

"Thankfully Seth came to us and exposed his father. I dread to think where your father and I would be today if he hadn't. We owe our marriage to that young man. He was a blessing in our darkest storm."

The gratitude in her mother's words soothed and reassured Nikki.

"He came all the way to Ohio just to tell you of his father's plot." Nikki affirmed feeling her heart soften a bit.

"Yes, he came in long enough to meet with us and to give us the file with your name on it. He made us promise not to tell you. He didn't want to upset you any further and knew that you'd never forgive him," Elaine said.

"You still have the file?" Nikki asked holding her breath hoping she'd have an opportunity one day to see just what was inside it.

"No, we burned it years ago," Elaine said. "We didn't

want you to find it one day. Seth protected us. We protected you."

"Thank you, Mom. Seems I have an apology to make," Nikki said unsure of how she felt. Her parents hid what Seth had done knowing how she'd felt about him. Even though it appeared he didn't care enough to see her when he'd had the chance, she understood why.

"Nicole, you know I've never interfered with your life choices. But if Seth Jermaine is single and still in love with you, , don't let this chance for happiness slip away," her mother suggested strongly when what she was really telling Nikki was not to throw this opportunity away.

"I won't, Mom," Nikki promised. "Love you and Dad."

"We love you too, Nikki."

Nikki heard the connection between them break. Much like the way she thought she knew everything about Seth only to confirm his unbelievable yet true story.

Seth sat quietly in the gazebo while snowflakes twinkled around the curtain of Christmas lights. The winter wind blew off the mountains yet his coat hung open. He welcomed the cold.

He wanted it to penetrate his heart. He didn't want to feel the warmth and the emotions that were there. Feelings he thought had died thirty years ago only to realize they'd been lying dormant until he saw Nikki again.

He didn't blame her for asking him to leave. How could he? He hadn't been man enough to stand up to his father back then and come back for her as promised.

Was he man enough now to win back her heart? And her trust?

He'd have to be if he wanted to regain her friendship before it was time for him to leave. And leaving was the last thing he wanted to do without knowing where he and Nikki stood with each other.

Exhaling, Seth stood for a moment allowing the frigid air to penetrate his lungs before returning to the inn. Satisfied with the slight sting of the cold air, he trudged up the path to the inn.

"Have you seen Chef Jermaine?" he heard as he stomped the snow off his boots just before ambling through the doorway. Nikki stood at the front desk, her back to him.

"I'm right here, Mrs. Reed," he replied huskily over her shoulder then put a short, respectable distance between them.

"Oh!" she exclaimed turning around, her eyes full of surprise. "What were you doing outside in this weather and at this time of night? The slopes aren't even open. Don't you know how dangerous that is?"

"Needed time to clear my head and plan for the arrival of the wedding party," he lied shrugging off his snow dusted coat. "I'd forgotten how much the crisp mountain air can do that. Last I checked the gazebo wasn't in the danger zone."

"I see. Well, that's what I'd like to talk to you about," she answered her cheeks turning a pretty shade of soft petal pink.

"The mountain air? Or the danger zone?" Seth teased, knowing full well what she really meant. He couldn't give any indication of what he hoped would happen between them. A reconciliation when all was said and done would be totally up to her and her alone.

"Anything you ask," Seth answered stepping closer, his voice low. "Your office then? Or back to your apartment?"

"I'm referring to the wedding! What did you think I meant, Seth?" she huffed as he followed in the wake of her light lavender scent. "My office will do quite nicely."

She really doesn't want to know what I think. Seth sensed she was being as untruthful with her feelings as he was. Maybe she was about to set ground rules he'd find hard pressed to follow. He didn't want any rules between them. Whatever happened had to come naturally as it did thirty years ago. But he'd do his best to gain her trust and to do as she wished. Even if it meant keeping things professional between them.

Seth walked into the office a few steps behind Nikki. A part of him couldn't wait to hear what she really wanted to talk about. While another part dreaded what she'd have to say.

"Please close the door and have a seat," Nikki instructed nonchalantly as she sat in one of the comfortable chairs.

Hmmm, talk about the wedding my eye. He was surprised when she hadn't settled in the chair behind her desk. It would have been the safest barrier for her to hide behind.

Maybe this is a good sign, he afforded himself the hopeful thought because at this moment he had nothing to lose. *Nothing ventured. Nothing gained. Isn't that the saying?*

"What's up, Nikki?" he asked closing the door, then turning to face her. "Not long ago you kicked me out of your apartment before I had a chance to explain further. Now you want to talk in your office?"

She's nervous about something, he thought watching the way she absentmindedly twisted the ends of her hair around a finger.

"I do apologize for being so rude twice in one day to you. It was hard for me to accept everything you told me earlier," she said. "I don't know, maybe I haven't gotten over the shock of you being here after all these years as well."

Not as shocked as I was to see you.

"Stop playing coy and tell me what's going on, Nikki." Seth didn't dare move any closer. He opted instead to keep the table between them. If he had the urge to be next to her at least the heavy piece of furniture would be a barrier.

"I'd like to call a truce while you are here," she said so quietly he wasn't sure if he'd actually heard her correctly.

"A truce?" Seth asked, forcing the smile from his face. "Why and what are the conditions?"

"The why should be clear enough. We are going to have to work together on some level. And I talked to my mom. She confirmed what you told me and filled in a few missing details," Nikki said looking down at her hands. "I wish I had known then the reason why you never followed up on your promise. It might have changed the way I felt all these years."

"I made your parents promise to never tell you. I didn't want you dragged into my family drama," Seth said solemnly, then chuckled. "And believe me, there was a lot of it back then."

"Mom told me as much," Nikki said softly her expression sad.

"Between my father's underhanded way of doing what

he considered business and having to go through with the wedding, I couldn't bring you into it."

"The truth would have been better than the lie," Nikki said, her gaze matching his with a painful intensity that stabbed at his heart.

"But equally hurtful," he said giving up and moving closer to her. "I didn't want to live with seeing the pain on your face that I see now. It was hard enough as it was."

"I loved you, Seth. I would have endured anything to be with you," she confessed looking at him with tears glistening in her eyes.

And I never stopped loving you, he thought even as his heart broke seeing the deepening pain reach her tear filled eyes. This was exactly why he hadn't wanted her to know about his father's way of doing business. He didn't want her to know the shame he'd felt when he'd finally realized what kind of a man his father was.

"Even shame? Ridicule? Constantly being hounded by reporters?" Seth asked praying that she'd say no but knowing she'd say yes.

"Love, true love, does that to a person. Makes them accept the one they love with all the baggage that comes with them." Nikki smiled, wiping the single tear trailing down her cheek.

"I'm not so sure about that, Nikki," Seth mumbled unsure if he believed in the power of true love anymore.

"Do you agree to a truce then?" Nikki's voice was hopeful.

"Only on one condition," Seth offered, looking her straight in the eyes. He wanted to see if she was open to a possible future with him.

"What's that?" Nikki asked.

"That during this 'truce' we see if there is a future for us," Seth said firmly. "Neither one of us has a commitment to another and since we are going to be together for a few weeks it's the perfect opportunity."

"Let's first see if we can be friends again," Nikki suggested.

"Agreed, after all it's a good place to start." Seth felt more hopeful than he'd been for more years than he'd care to count.

CHAPTER FIVE

The Adams-Hathaway wedding party was due to arrive today and there'd been no time for Nikki to even take a breath much less anything else. The past few days since she'd last had a chance to speak with Seth for more than a few words seemed eons ago. She barely had time to be social with her staff, let alone a past love that may or may not be a future love.

She didn't have time for affairs of the heart. She had a checklist to go over one more time before any of the guests arrived. The rooms needed one last go through after the thorough cleaning they'd all undergone the past few days. The pantry needed to be stocked, which Nikki could only presume Seth had already taken care of. The inn's car and shuttle needed to be gassed up and ready to make the drive down the mountain to the airport as soon as the calls came in. Snow removal had to be done as well as the salt and sand scattered on the walkways.

She always got this way when a large group was sched-uled. She couldn't eat right. Barely slept with worry something might go wrong. Which it rarely, if ever, did. This wedding was the event of the year and could put her little inn back on the map so to speak.

Nikki leaned back in her chair. *Just a minute, that's all I need is one minute to clear my mind,* she thought closing her eyes. The list she'd held in her hand drifted to the floor. The soft Christmas music playing on the inn's speaker faded away. And for a few delicious minutes she was that small town, Ohio girl who'd fallen in love with a boy from the Big Apple.

"Ms. Reed?"

"Huh?" Nikki opened her sleepy eyes. "What time is it, Ashley?"

"It's around ten."

"Ten!? It can't be that late," Nikki stated looking for her checklist.

"Thomas has left with the shuttle to pick up the bridal party," Ashley said grinning. "How long have you been asleep?"

"Longer than I should have," she said shuffling through the papers. "Have you seen my checklist, I can't find it."

"Hum, check the floor," Ashley said.

"How long has Thomas been gone?" Nikki picked up the list then pushed out of the chair. She couldn't afford to get that comfortable again. At least not until the wedding was over and everyone had left.

"They should be arriving any minute now," Asley answered.

"Have you told Chef Jermaine yet?"

"I was going there next."

"I'll go. I need a good strong cup of coffee and I hope he's brewed a pot of it." Nikki walked with Ashley into the lobby, the checklist rolled up in her hand. "Let everyone know the guests will be arriving soon."

"I already have, Ms. Reed," Ashley said sliding into her seat behind the front desk.

"Of course you have. What would I do without you, Ashley." Nikki smiled and continued through the dining room to the kitchen.

She stood in the doorway amazed at the buzz of activity. Seth and the kitchen staff were working like a well-oiled machine. Nikki felt like a proud momma watching her staff follow his direction quickly and efficiently.

"I heard you might be needing this," Seth said, placing a hot cup of coffee in her hand as he took her elbow leading her to a small table on the outskirts of the bustle of the kitchen.

"I don't have time for this, Seth," she protested even as her stomach rumbled with need from the aroma of ginger-bread pancakes, eggs, bacon, and toast.

"You will make time. In case you haven't noticed, we don't have time to pick you up and take you to the hospital if you pass out from exhaustion," he instructed practically pushing her down in the chair. "Now eat!"

"Let me make this clear, I'm eating because I'm hungry, not because you are insisting that I do," Nikki said buttering a piece of toast.

"Anything you say, Ms. Reed," Seth winked, then went back to giving the staff instruction on the brunch they were all preparing.

Nikki watched him move about with precision. Not once did he raise his voice. If someone didn't understand him, he walked them through it with the gentle encouragement of a father.

She couldn't take her eyes off him and her heart flipped when he caught her gaze and gave her another wink.

Seth stood at a counter watching Nikki as he prepared corned beef brisket for later. He knew, even before Nikki had strolled into the kitchen, that she hadn't been eating right. He overheard the kitchen staff commenting on how she was going to give them all a scare. When he asked Gabby about it, the sous-chef told him that Nikki barely slept or ate when there was a big party booked at the inn. That once she actually passed out in the lobby. An ambulance had been called, only to have her chase them away after they'd examined her and her vitals were normal.

Gabby told him that since then Chef Winston would always have a meal waiting for her in the morning and strong coffee as well. Her routine was to go to her office first, then try to sneak into the kitchen to make sure everything was moving alone. Gabby said that after that day Nikki had fainted, the staff made it a point to check on her throughout the day. There hadn't been another incident since.

He wasn't about to let anything happen to her while he was here. As long as it was within his power, he wouldn't fail her again.

"Ms. Reed," Ashley called out from the kitchen doorway.

"Yes?" Nikki mumbled.

"Thomas has called," Ashley said from across the room.

"Is he on his way?" Nikki called out, an anxious look on her face.

"Why don't you just come in, sit down and have a muffin while you tell Ms. Reed what it is that Thomas said," Seth suggested, placing a muffin and pad of butter on a dessert plate.

"Oh, no I couldn't! I'm not to go into the kitchen," Ashy insisted.

"Of course you can," Seth insisted kindly, handing her the plate. "I need to make sure the staff can hear me over your shouting."

"Come Ashley, and tell me what is going on," Nikki invited.

Ashley walked slowly across the room and sat down at the table with Nikki. They talked quietly as they ate. He wondered if something was wrong, but then dismissed the thought as Ashley was too calm for something horrible to have happened. After several minutes, Ashley nodded then left the kitchen her partially eaten muffin in her hand.

"Is everything okay?" Seth asked, wiping his greasy hands down the once white apron.

"Yes. Thomas is waiting for the next plane to come in before bringing the group up the mountain," Nikki answered.

"Make sense if they are close together," Seth agreed.

"The next plane lands in about thirty minutes, so it will save both time and energy. The first group was happy to wait for the bride and groom, the wedding planner, and wedding photographer," Nikki smiled. "We have a good hour or so before they all arrive. Thanks for breakfast, Chef."

"It was my pleasure. Take a few muffins back to your office in case you need something to munch on later," Seth said setting a plate of blueberry muffins in front of her.

"Thank you," she said then strolled out of the kitchen with a bit more energy than when she'd arrived.

"Thank you, Chef," Gabby said from near one of the ovens.

"Listen up everyone. I want to thank each and every one of you for your hard work this morning; you all did great," Seth said meaning every word. A kitchen is only as good as its staff, and no one could convince him otherwise. "It is going to get hectic once the wedding party and guests arrive, so please take a few minutes and grab something to eat. You'll need the fuel.

"And thank you for allowing me to take care of Ms. Reed. If you hadn't told me how she handles things, I wouldn't have had anything ready."

"If you don't mind me being candid, Chef," Gabby said being the spokesperson for the staff.

"No, of course not. In fact, I welcome it," Seth remarked wanting Gabby and the rest of the staff to know they could tell him anything.

"We all can tell how much you care for Ms. Reed, but with all due respect if you hurt her, you'll have mutiny on your hands," Gabby threatened, her eyes full of promised daggers.

"Believe me, hurting Ms. Reed is that last thing I plan to do," Seth answered. "Now grab some food and then let's get back to work. We're going to have twenty or more hungry people to feed sooner than you think."

"Yes, Chef," everyone said in unison.

Seth watched these people who obviously loved Nikki Reed as much, if not more, than he did. And he was going to make sure that she knew it before there wasn't time to do so.

Nikki sat in her office savoring the delicious muffins. The blueberries were fresh, not frozen. She could tell from the way they'd held up during the baking; no soggy bottom on these muffins. She may not be a chef, but she'd learned something from Chef Winston over the years. In some instances she wondered if he wasn't preparing her to pick his successor once he finally retired.

"Would Seth be interested in replacing Miles at some point?" She wondered even if Seth did have plans to return to New York City after the wedding. "Don't be daft! He must have a restaurant or two to run. He couldn't very well run it from here and be the inn's chef as well."

"Still talking to yourself I hear."

Nikki's breath caught in her throat. "How long have you been standing there?"

"Not long enough or I'd know what you were muttering about," Seth said, leaning against the door jam, with a carafe in one hand and a cup in the other.

"Inn business, nothing more," Nikki lied hoping he hadn't heard anything she'd said. She didn't want him to think she was planning to lure him away from the city life he most likely thrived on.

"Care if I join you? Or would I be interrupting?" Seth didn't wait for her to invite him in. He strolled across the room oozing that youthful confidence she'd found so attractive.

"Please do," she said sweeping her hand toward the chair across the desk from her. "Is that more of the coffee I had in the kitchen?"

"Would you like me to top you off?" he said nodding.

"Do I really have to ask? And if you don't mind, can you keep the coffee coming all day? I have a feeling I'm going to need it." She grinned. "I must admit, the breakfast you made was exactly what I needed."

"You have your staff to thank for that," Seth said filling her cup then sitting down across from her.

"What did my staff say?" she asked wondering what gossip about her had been going around the inn.

"First of all, the staff – all the staff – love and respect you. Did you know that?" Seth said settling back into the chair that looked as if it was made just for him.

"I had a feeling, but I try not to take people and their feelings for granted. It never works out and the possibility of being wrong is not something I want to experience with my staff," Nikki said feeling the shield she'd left down a few days ago start to slide back into place.

"They were worried about you not getting enough rest and that you weren't eating right, if at all," Seth said. "Since I can ease their minds on part of their worries, I arranged to have breakfast waiting for you this morning. And whether you like it or not, there will be breakfast on your desk each morning."

"Along with coffee?" Nikki grinned over the top of the now steamy cup.

"Definitely along with coffee. As well as juice and water

to stay hydrated," Seth assured, glancing past her shoulder. "How long has it been snowing like that?"

Nikki sucked in a breath and turned to look out the window. It was snowing. Hard and heavy.

"I have no idea, but it can't be a good sign," she said, getting up to take a closer look as her phone rang.

"Gingerbread Inn, Nikki Reed here," she said with practiced cheerfulness. "Thomas, slow down."

"They are closing the road up the mountain, Ms. Reed," Thomas said, his voice a bit anxious. "The snow started coming down harder right after I called earlier. Since then the weather conditions have caused the state patrol to close the road until it stops and they can get it clear."

"Did they say how long it will be?" Nikki asked chewing her bottom lip.

"They say the road to the inn should be cleared by late afternoon tomorrow," Thomas said doubtfully. "I took the initiative of booking the guests into the hotel here in town at the expense of the inn."

"Good thinking. Have all their meals covered by the inn as well. In the meantime, I'll turn on the scanner and try to keep informed on the conditions. If you hear anything new let me know," Nikki instructed a bit relieved her guests would be safe in town. "And Thomas, thank you for taking care of our guests."

"You're welcome, Ms. Reed. I'll have them safely to the inn as soon as I can tomorrow," Thomas said then the call cut off.

"What's wrong?" Seth queried.

"The road to the inn is closed and the wedding party are

staying at the local hotel," Nikki said softly. "Thomas will let me know tomorrow when he can bring them to the inn."

"I better get back to the kitchen and put a few things on hold," Seth said. "You did the right thing, Nikki."

"I didn't do anything. Thomas knew what to do," Nikki said staring at the snow falling heavier outside the window. "And he did exactly what I would have told him to do."

"I'll make soup and bread for the staff to have today," Seth offered coming up behind her. "I'll bring you some as well, if you'd like."

"Perfect. Thank you, Seth," she said turning into his arms. She allowed herself to feel his warmth for a moment before stepping aside. "I'll see you later."

She grabbed her coat and walked away, leaving him to figure out if he'd done something wrong or not.

CHAPTER SIX

Seth stood in Nikki's office watching as she slipped her coat on and walked away from him. The way she'd lingered in his arms and then abruptly stepped away should have made him wonder what he'd done wrong. But it didn't.

What it did do was make him want to go after her even though he felt she needed to clear her head and regroup without distraction. The last thing she needed was for him to play hero. That privilege had been dissolved years ago.

Returning to the kitchen he was pleased to find the staff had begun to put the prepped food away. He smiled hearing Gabby give direction in a calm manner.

That girl is going to make an excellent chef one day, he thought clearing his throat.

Gabby turned looking like she'd been caught with her hand in the cookie jar. "Sorry Chef, I thought it best to get everything in the refrigerator before things spoiled."

"You did the right thing, Gabby. I can see why Chef Winston thinks highly of you," he said surveying the work of the staff. "It appears you have the matter well in hand. Just one question."

"Yes, Chef," Gabby said beaming with pride.

"Where would Ms. Reed go to mull things over?" Seth asked grabbing a couple of thermoses and filling them with hot cocoa that had been prepared for the now delayed guests.

"Well it depends on what the problem is." Gabby glanced at him placing the wrapped brisket in the freezer. "If it's personal she usually will take refuge in the gazebo."

"And if it's not personal?"

"If it has anything to do with the inn, she will sometimes head over to the lift chairs. She'll either ride them up and down until she has a solution for the problem," Gabby answered. "Or sit for a while. It all depends on whether or not the slopes are busy."

"Even with the snow falling as it is?" Seth was concerned that if Nikki followed her usual routine she'd get lost in the snow on her way to the lifts.

"I would check the gazebo first," Gabby answered wiping down the counter.

His mind was made up. He was going after Nikki and he didn't care if she wanted him to or not. He needed to make sure she was okay.

"Thank you," Seth said surveying the kitchen once more. "Everyone, please be sure you make yourself something to eat. And thank you all for being, well, at the sake of sounding corny, for being the wonderful staff that you are."

Seth jogged out of the kitchen and through the inn until he reached his room. He opened the door in haste, gabbed his coat, and slipped it on as he jogged back through the lobby and out the door.

"Nikki," he yelled through the falling snow as he made his way toward the gazebo.

His heart sank when he reached the empty structure. *Where are you, Nikki,* he wondered retracing his steps back to the inn.

Standing under the shelter of the front door overhang, Seth peered through the snow. His worry for Nikki's safety increased. Any hope of finding her near the inn nearly expired until he finally noticed the door to the shed near the parking lot partially open.

"With any luck," he muttered, tucking the thermoses into his coat. Head down against the wind, Seth trudged through the snow and cold until he reached the shed door.

Squeezing through the opening, he called out, "Nikki, are you in here?"

"Yes, where else would I be in this weather if I'm not inside the inn?" she asked from under the roof of the green Trailblazer plow.

"Oh, I don't know. The lift maybe? Or are you planning to plow the drive?" he sputtered, sliding into the passenger seat. "I brought hot cocoa."

"Thank you," she said opening the offered thermos and pouring the steaming cocoa into the cup. "Gabby told you about the lift, didn't she?"

"Yes, but only because I asked. They all care about you, Nikki," Seth said not bothering with the cup and drinking straight from the thermos.

"It's too dangerous to go to the lifts so I came here."

Nikki cradled the cup in her gloved hands. "Only thing missing are marshmallows."

"You mean these?" Seth pulled out a small bag of mini marshmallows from his coat pocket.

"You thought of everything." Nikki giggled, depositing several into her cocoa. "Now it's perfect."

"Not quite," he said looking at her, waiting for her to look at him. "What are you doing out here, Nikki?"

"Running," she said looking at him, her eyes glistening.

"From what?" Seth asked hoping it wasn't him yet knowing it was a possibility.

"Everything?" Nikki shrugged.

"You mean me, don't you?" Seth noticed the slight nod of her head.

NIKKI HELD HIS GAZE. How could she tell him that it wasn't really because of him. It was because of the way it felt to be in his arms, even for a fraction of a moment. She didn't dare stay that close to him. To lean on him. To need his strength.

"Not really, but maybe," she finally admitted.

"I'm sorry," he apologized softly.

"No need to apologize, Seth. It's not you, it's me." Nikki touched his arm lightly then quickly withdrew. It was too intimate of a gesture for her right now.

"Now that sounds like a cliché way of breaking up with someone." Seth chuckled.

"Yes, I guess it does if we were dating, or something," Nikki said feeling her heart ache. If only they were dating again things might be simpler. Then again, most likely not.

"That's true," Seth agreed. "What would it hurt if we at least talked about it?"

Her breath escaped her body. He couldn't be serious. After all these years? After the nights of crying herself to sleep? Years of wondering what she'd done or hadn't done?

"You know what they say about mixing pleasure with business. It just doesn't work out the way you think," Nikki replied half believing her own words. If she wasn't convinced why should she expect Seth to be?

"I'm willing to at least talk about it, aren't you?" Seth asked under his breath. "Or are all the feelings you once had for me dead and buried, because I can tell you with certainty that mine for you are not."

"Seth, I'm a widow. An older widow, not a fanciful girl of twenty," Nikki pointed out fighting back those dark shadows of grief.

"And I'm a fifty something divorced man," Seth countered. "Is there a rule people like us can't have a second chance at happiness? That we aren't allowed to write our second chapter of love?"

"Seth, I'm not sure it's possible," Nikki answered wanting so much to say yes to the idea of the two of them starting again. "Let's be real about this. You'll be going back to New York City when the wedding is over. I don't think I could handle the heartache again. Twice in a lifetime is more than enough for anyone."

She jumped when he took her hand in his squeezing it lightly.

"I'm not going to say that I know how you feel, because it would be half a lie," Seth said. "I do know what it is like to lose at love, but I have no idea about losing the one you loved and gave your life to forever.

"I can't speak for your late husband but I can honestly say that if it were me I'd want the woman I loved to go on living. To find love again."

"Yes, that's what Tony would want." Nikki wiped away her tears with a gloved hand. "I don't know if I can trust—"

"Me not to leave again?" Seth finished.

"I'm sorry, Seth, but exactly." Nikki sniffed gathering what strength she had to fight the feelings she'd been having since he walked into the inn.

"What can I do to convince you that I won't leave you again?" Seth nearly begged

"I don't know." Nikki looked at him seeing the pain on his face. She had to at least throw him a bone. "Can we take it slow and see how we feel when this wedding is over? I know it's only a week, but by then you may realize that you're not willing to give up the excitement of New York City for being stuck in the middle of nowhere at a small mountain inn named after a Christmas cookie."

"As long as you are willing to give it a try, that's all I can ask," Seth said, putting an arm around her shoulder. "And once you realize that I am now a man of my word, I'm going to show you just how much you mean to me."

"Well, on that note," Nikki said smiling up at him. "I need to get back inside. I've got to check the weather and see when my guests might be arriving."

. . .

SETH SCREWED the cups back on the thermoses then helped Nikki out of the snowplow. Side by side they walked out of the shed and back to the inn.

"The snow has stopped," Seth noted as they moved closer to the inn. "A good sign, right?"

"Definitely a good sign," Nikki agreed, her step quickening until they reached the front door.

Seth held the door open, allowing Nikki to enter ahead of him. It was quiet but festive with Christmas music playing softly. For the first time, he noticed the perfect tree standing in a corner near the expanse of windows. The lights flickered off and on in time to the music.

"I've forgotten the feel of Christmas joy," he said, shrugging off his coat. "You've captured it fully, Nikki."

"Thank you, but my staff deserves all the credit. I give them full control over the decorations." Nikki's pride for her staff was evident in every word.

"Well, it shows and I've no doubt this is why Kenna Blackstone suggested the Gingerbread Inn for the Adams-Hathaway destination wedding." Seth knew Kenna had worked hard to convince the couple to have their winter wedding here instead of in the heart of New York City.

"I certainly hope I don't disappoint anyone. And on that note, I'll see you for dinner then," Nikki said walking back to her office. "I'm looking forward to that soup you spoke of earlier today. I am chilled to the bone."

Smiling, Seth returned to his room and for the first time felt a lightness in his heart. A feeling of hope his life was on the right path once again after so many years.

"Now which soup to make," he muttered searching the recipes archived in his mind. "Something quick, hardy and filling. Hmmm," he pondered closing the door to his room and making his way to the kitchen. "I've got it!"

Seth bustled around the kitchen prepping yellow onions, celery and garlic as sweet potatoes boiled on the stove. Once they were tender, he pureed them with chicken stock as the other ingredients were sauteing in a stock pot with olive oil.

Adding the puree to the pot with the remaining chicken stock, Seth brought the mixture to a boil. He started making the quick rising bread as the bisque simmered, stirring often. After an hour and a half he added the cream and sherry to the smooth mixture.

Satisfied with how the bisque tasted, he pulled out the bread from the oven. Placing the stock pot, bread, butter and several bowls, saucers and silverware on a cart alongside bottles of water and a pot of coffee, he rolled it out to the dining room.

After setting up the banquet table, he went into the lobby where to his surprise the inn's staff sat around the fireplace chatting.

"I hope that deliciousness floating through the air means it's time to eat," Ashley chirped from behind the front desk. "If not, you'll have a lot of explaining to do."

Seth laughed out loud. "All I can say to that is you'd better go eat before the soup cools."

"Ms. Reed, come and eat," Ashley called in the direction of the office's open door.

"I'll be there in a minute," Nikki answered from her office.

Seth followed the staff into the dining room lagging behind in case Nikki came in. Once everyone had gone through, he filled bowls with bisque for both him and Nikki, as well as a plate with a several thick pieces of bread and then hot steaming coffee.

"Good news!" Nikki said, walking into the dining room. "The state patrol says the roads will be cleared by morning. I spoke with Thomas and he'll have our guests here in time for breakfast. Can you manage it, Chef Jermaine?" she asked.

"I think so," Seth said then looked over at his staff clustered around a table together. "I've got an amazing staff to work with."

"Good, I'm glad that you have found them more than adequate," Nikki said spooning soup into her mouth.

"That, Ms. Reed, is an understatement and you know it." Seth laughed, even though he knew the kitchen would be chaotic in the morning. For once, he looked forward to it.

CHAPTER SEVEN

Nikki stared at the contract and guest list in front of her. No matter how much she tried, her mind kept going back to last night. She had guests arriving this morning and all she could think about was Seth.

Being around Seth these last few days had rekindled something she'd never thought she'd ever feel again. How could she feel this way after only a few days? Yet, she did, and it scared and delighted her at the same time.

When she ran away from him, she wasn't sure where she was going. All she knew was she had to be alone for a while. She hadn't expected him to come looking for her.

And find her no less.

"If I had made sure the door was completely closed, he never would have looked in the shed," she muttered leaning back in the chair a small smile seeping onto her face.

He'd been kind and sweet finding her hiding place. Thoughtful as well with the thermos of hot chocolate and marshmallows he'd brought with him.

In those sweet moments it felt like the hands of time had turned back. Then she realized they weren't kids anymore, but adults with emotional baggage.

Did she have the strength to deal with his past along with her own?

She trusted him. Was it really enough to give her heart to him once more?

She felt they could be friends once he went back to New York City, but would she allow him to take her heart with him? Nikki didn't know if she was willing, or even able, to take that plunge again. Especially now when she'd finally settled into a nice routine of life.

Tap, tap, on the door followed by the *swish* of it opening drew her attention away from her musing. Nikki looked up to see who needed her now. When her gaze met Seth's, she knew she'd give him everything.

"I brought you breakfast and coffee," Seth grinned placing the tray on her desk in front of her. "I've got a breakfast buffet set up in the dining room for the guests when they arrive."

"Are you sure that'll be adequate enough?" she asked. "I don't want to get off on the wrong foot with this group. They are essential to my making the inn what it once was… a place where families came all year round, especially during the holidays."

"Trust me, Kenna Blackstone chose the Gingerbread Inn for its quaintness. If she'd thought New York City would have been the perfect place for this wedding, she'd have booked it," Seth assured her with confidence. "I've made sure when they step through those doors, Christmas memories will strike them all."

"How?" Nikki asked knowing there was only one way to bring those kinds of memories and Chef Winston wasn't there to create them with his gingerbread recipes.

"With Gabby's help," Seth said a twinkle in his eye. "She knows Chef Winston's recipes so well that I handed some of the buffet items over to her."

"The inn's signature aroma." Nikki smiled.

"Yes, how could it be any other way?" Seth said sitting down. "Gabby should have the title of head chef. She knows what she's doing. But she admires and respects Chef Winston too much to ask for a promotion."

"Are you sure she can handle the responsibility?" Nikki asked knowing Miles would be throwing a fit if he knew his sous-chef was assisting in the running of his kitchen.

"Ms. Reed," Ashley chirped from the open doorway. "Thomas called and left a message. They should be on their way."

"Thank you, Ashley," she said, starting to push away from her desk only to feel Seth's presence fall upon her.

"Nikki, I am not going to let you leave the room until you at least eat those eggs, a piece of toast, and a few slices of bacon."

"I don't have time—"

"You have at least thirty minutes. You aren't going to be any good to anyone if you faint because you haven't eaten."

"Will this do?" she asked, piling bacon and eggs between two pieces of buttered toast.

"Yes. And to answer your question, Gabby is more than able to handle the kitchen."

"Good. And for your information, I will eat on the run. I've got a wedding party arriving," she said, taking an exaggerated bite out of the sandwich as she squeezed by him.

SETH HUSTLED through the dining room and into the kitchen. Looking around he felt a sense of pride flip into him. He'd only been with this crew for a few days but they'd stepped up to the plate for him. And he couldn't have asked for more.

"Can I have your attention please," he requested loudly. Once everyone stood still he drew a deep breath.

"The wedding party is on their way and should arrive within twenty minutes," he informed in a more normal volume. "Please make sure everything in the dining room is hot and ready to receive a good number of people.

"Gabby, I am putting you in charge of making sure the food is prepared properly and timely," Seth instructed doing his best to suppress a grin.

"Yes, Chef," Gabby called out from her station.

"Good. Now let's make the inn smell like home on Christmas Day," Seth said, tying his apron around his waist.

The bustle in the kitchen resumed. He heard Gabby give direction gently but with a firmness some chefs never master. He'd been right in his assessment of her; she'd make a great head chef and eventually an executive chef one day. Hopefully he'd be able to help her achieve it if that was what she wanted.

"Gabby, are those dishes of Chef Winston's about done?" Seth asked, pulling the beef out from the refrigerator.

"Ten minutes on the bread and five on the mulled wine," Gabby answered as she continued chopping ginger.

"Let's make this the best brunch these New Yorkers have ever had," Seth encouraged, cutting the slab of beef into cubes. He was going to give the guests some comfort food meant to be savored on cold winter days. Nothing could do that better than a good hardy stew with warm custard for dessert followed up with a hot toddy. "They will be amazed by how eating at a little inn in the mountains is so much better than eating in a big city restaurant."

"Yes, Chef!" the staff called out.

"Chef Jermaine, the wedding party is about five minutes from the inn," Nikki called nervously from the outskirts of the kitchen.

Seth looked up from his meal preparation. If a picture painted a thousand words then the one he saw before him spoke volumes. Nikki was worried as all get out. Dropping what he was doing, he walked quickly to her.

"It smells fabulous in here," Nikki said just below her breath. "Reminds me of home on Christmas morning."

"That's what we were going for," Seth smiled, leaning into her. "We've got things handled here; you go and take care of your guests. They'll want to know who will be responsible for them having had a marvelous stay."

"One could hope," she said with apprehension in her voice.

"I know these kind of people, Nikki. I have complete confidence in you. They are going to fall in love with the inn just as you and I did thirty years ago," he whispered for her ears only. When she looked up at him with a softness in her eyes, he kissed her gently on the forehead. He took her hand in his, rubbing a thumb across the top.

"Ms. Reed, the car is a few minutes away."

And just like that the magic he'd felt broke and fell between them. Nikki smiled then turned and hurried away chattering to Ashley.

"Okay let's get everything into the dining room," Seth called out, helping his kitchen staff where he could. He wasn't one of those chefs who stood by and watched as everyone did the work. He was right in there with them. If they failed, they failed together.

Taking a deep breath, Nikki watched the inn's SUV pull up to the doors. "Here we go," she said more to herself than to anyone around her.

As the last of the passengers stepped away from the vehicle, the door opened with a *swoosh* and the scent of fresh air.

"Welcome to The Gingerbread Inn," Nikki greeted with a smile on her face.

"Ms. Reed?" the woman asked as she gazed around the lobby.

"Yes, Miss…?" Nikki asked holding out her hand.

"Blackstone, Kenna Blackstone," Kenna answered accepting Nikki's hand with a firm grip. "This is *exactly* how I imagined it to be. The pictures really don't do justice to the feeling I got walking in the door. They are going to love it!" Kenna continued in an upbeat cheerleader kind of way.

"The bride and groom?" Nikki asked wondering if it was that simple.

"And the smell of the holidays the moment you walk in the door," Kenna continued as if she hadn't heard the question. "It takes me back to my childhood days."

"Miss Blackstone, as soon as everyone's bags have been brought in, I will show you to your rooms," Nikki said watching the wedding participants assemble in the lobby.

"Kimberly! Charles! What do you think?" Kenna asked bubbily, turning toward a young couple Nikki could only assess were the bride and groom.

They looked to be in their twenties. Maybe not long out of college for they still held that scholarly look about them.

And very much in love if holding hands and giving longing looks to one another were any indication.

"Charles, it smells just like Granny's home on Christmas Eve," the young lady said her eyes filled with the glee of a child.

"And so, it does, Kimberly," the young man agreed, leading the way over to the window and the large Blue Spruce decorated to perfection. "Look! You can almost see the very top of the mountain from here. And the light twinkles off the snow like in the movies. It's so magical."

"Come and meet our hostess," Kenna encouraged, as the couple turned back toward the rest of the party milling around. "Kimberly, Charles, this is Ms. Reed. Ms. Reed this is Kimberly Adams and Charles Hathaway, the bride and groom."

"I have been looking forward to meeting both of you," Nikki greeted shaking each of their hands. "And of course, being a part of your wedding day as well. From the sidelines of course."

"Thank you," the couple said in unison.

"And now that you are all here, let me show you all to the dining room where Chef Jermaine and his staff have prepared a heartwarming lunch for you." Nikki turned and led the way to the dining room where steam rose from several serving chafing dishes. She was thankful Seth had made her eat something earlier or she'd have embarrassed herself with stomach rumblings.

"Thank you, Ms. Reed." Kenna nodded, herding the large group toward the banquet table of steaming food. "After a night in the small hotel, everyone is ready to settle in for the duration."

"Then I shall leave you to it." Nikki smiled, leaving her guests to fill their stomachs and relax.

"Thomas, please put Ms. Adams's bags in the large room on the second floor overlooking the mountains. Then Mr. Hathaway's bags can go into one of the others but at the opposite end of the hall. Miss Blackstone's bags will go into the room opposite Mr. Hathaway's. Everyone else's can go into the rooms as listed here," Nikki instructed handing Thomas the list of where everyone was to go. "Thank you, Thomas."

"Yes, Ms. Reed." Thomas nodded, loading up the baggage cart.

"Ashley, is everyone checked in?" Nikki asked as the door opened and a beautiful brunette with long flowing hair and legs that didn't seem to end walked in. "I guess not," she whispered.

"Welcome to The Gingerbread Inn. Are you with the wedding party?" Nikki asked feeling a chill up her spine when the lady approaching gave her a hard cold stare.

"Yes," the woman chirped pulling off her hat and gloves. The camera hanging around her neck frosted over slightly from the difference in temperature. "I am the photographer."

"Your name?" Nikki asked wondering what had happened to this woman to mar any beauty within.

"Sinclair," the woman answered. "You have a beautiful place here. So many great photo op possibilities once it warms up."

"Well, I'm afraid you'll have to wait until the spring thaw for warmth. Until then…"

"I don't find anyone with that last name, Ms. Reed," Ashley said, glancing up at Nikki.

"What was your name again? We can't seem to find you on our reservation listing," Nikki asked.

"Oh of course, Kenna may have added me onto her own reservation," the woman answered, swinging back around. "I'm Payton Sinclair-Jermaine."

Nikki swallowed hard. Her rival all those years ago stood in front of her in all her expensive New York City fashion like a beacon from the past.

Seth's ex-wife was here to complicate her life once again.

CHAPTER EIGHT

"Payton! What are you doing here?" Seth exclaimed from the just beyond the lobby. He was both surprised and suspicious. How did she know he was here? He had checked with Kenna Blackstone as to who the photographer for the wedding was before he signed the contract as the chef. It was supposed to be someone from Drake's Digital Photography, not his ex-wife!

"Didn't Kenna tell you?" Payton asked turning her cold gaze from Nikki onto him.

"No, why should she?" Seth asked walking cautiously over to the desk. His dislike for this woman was beyond his comprehension sometimes. He didn't trust her.

"I thought she would let you know that because of a family emergency with Drake's, your ex was going to part of the wedding party, that's all," Payton replied, the smirk on her face something he all too well remembered.

"Have you met our hostess and owner of the Gingerbread Inn, Ms. Reed?" Seth placed himself between the two women who had each once been a part of his life. One he hoped would never be again. The other one he'd hoped there might be a future with.

"Yes, we've met," Nikki answered quickly, breaking the tension in the room and throwing him a questioning glance. "Miss Sinclair, I'll have your bags brought up to your room. In the meantime, I'm sure Chef Jermaine would be happy to escort you to the dining room. I understand there is a wonderful spread in there waiting to be devoured."

"Yes, well, I'm sure there are a number of things *Chef* Jermaine would like to devour," Payton taunted. "Or at least he did at one time, didn't you, Seth my love?"

"Payton, I suggest we keep personal feelings out of the equation. Once the wedding is over, then you can let your claws out," Seth scoffed, taking her by the elbow and tugging her toward the dining room.

"I don't know what game you are thinking of playing, but don't ruin the wedding or both of our reputations because of your pettiness," Seth warned knowing full well that he'd have to keep close to his ex-wife in order to protect Nikki. If Payton figured out just who Nikki was…

"Oh come now, Seth. You can't tell me you haven't made your move on the inn keeper. You've been here for a few days now, I'm sure you've had your fill of her," Payton said under her breath.

"You don't know anything about Ms. Reed, nor will you," Seth cautioned. "She's a professional and while she's friendly, which is required given she owns the Gingerbread Inn, she's anything but a fling. Unlike your latest. What is his name? Damon?"

"David, and I've moved on from him," Payton retorted. "In fact, you may have the chance to meet Robert while we are here. But only if I decide to give him permission to come, that is."

"Some people never change," Seth growled.

"I was kidding, Seth. I wanted to see if I could get a rise out of you, and it worked," Payton murmured. "I haven't been seeing anyone for well over a year now once I realized that I still have you in my heart."

"You what!?" Seth all but shouted, causing the guests in the dining room to stop eating and look their way.

"You are out of your ever-loving mind, Payton, if you think for one minute that I'd ever go back to you," he assured under his breath. "That piped up dream of yours will never come true, so you might as well just let it die and be buried—for good."

Nodding at the diners he promptly deposited Payton in front of the steaming dishes. He didn't want to deal with his ex-wife's lies and deceptions but knew if he didn't he'd not only tarnish his reputation he might lose his possibility of convincing Nikki to give them—him—a second chance.

What he needed right now to get through this wedding was a bit of Christmas magic.

NIKKI STOOD behind the desk trembling like a leaf. The last person she expected to ever meet in her lifetime was the woman who had stolen her happiness. But there she'd been standing in front of her with a smug look on her face and a better than you attitude.

"Ms. Reed, which room do these go up to?" Thomas asked, pulling the loaded luggage cart over.

"Oh, ah, put them in the same room as Ms. Blackstone's

until I figure out different arrangements," Nikki instructed. "I'll let Ms. Blackstone know of the situation myself."

"Yes, ma'am," Thomas nodded turning the cart toward the elevator.

"Thank you, Thomas." Nikki smiled turning back to the register to see which room she could put the former Mrs. Seth Jermaine in if need be. Although she knew exactly where she'd like to put her. On a plane with a one-way ticket to New York City and out of her life.

How could she even entertain the idea of starting something with Seth when it was clear as a starry night that his ex was far from being over him. She wasn't about to stand between them; it wouldn't be fair.

"Ms. Reed, you should grab something to eat," Ashley suggested placing a plate of food on the counter. "The stew is marvelous!"

"I will, later. Are you ready to take over for the rest of the day? I have all the room assignments here." She handed Ashley the list of guest rooms. "All of their bags are in their assigned rooms, so all they need to do is go settle in and relax."

"I've got this." Ashley smiled, spooning a large portion of stew into her mouth.

"Thank you. I'll be in my office for a few hours if anyone is looking for me." Nikki walked around the desk and straight to her office closing the door behind her.

Once inside she sank down into her chair and flipped open the folder marked "Adams/Hathaway." Shuffling through the papers in the folder, her mind kept seeing Payton Sinclair in a beautiful, diamond embossed wedding dress fit for a princess. And Seth standing at the end of a strip of white silk waiting for her. As Payton glided down the silk, she paused and looked Nikki straight in the eye and laughed before saying *"He's mine, not yours. He'll never be yours."*

Shoving the papers off the desk, she watched as the pages fluttered to the floor. "Get a grip, Nicole!" she scolded herself. "There's nothing here to be upset about and you know it."

Nikki knelt down on the floor and gathered the papers. Shuffling them into a reasonably neat pile, she stood only to drop them again.

"Now that was totally counterproductive, wouldn't you say?" Seth grinned rocking back on his heels.

"How long have you been standing there?" Nikki asked worried he'd heard more than she wanted anyone to ever hear. Taking a deep breath, she got back on the floor and collected the papers once more.

"Long enough to admire the way you scooped up those papers," he said offering her a hand up.

"That was far too long," she replied, reluctantly accepting his offer. "What can I do for you? Don't you have a kitchen to run and people to keep fed?"

"Gabby has the clean up handled so I thought we could have lunch," he said pushing the cart over to the desk.

"I really don't have time to eat, especially with you now that the wedding party and everyone has arrived. We must keep this professional, Seth," Nikki said hoping she was sounding more sincere than she felt.

"Nikki, you have to eat," Seth insisted placing covered bowls and plates on the desk. "Consider it a working lunch then since I want to go over the menu with you. I've already touched base with Kenna and she's open to everything I have in mind."

"All right then, Chef Jermaine," Nikki agreed knowing she wouldn't have put up much of a fuss to spend a few more minutes with him. Once the wedding preparations started they may not have any moments like this again. And when he left, they'd never have them.

"AFTER A LENGTHY CONVERSATION with Kenna and convincing her that in order to fully appreciate the experience of a winter destination wedding to the mountains, she's approved a rustic, yet elegant meal for the wedding reception," Seth advised pushing the napkin with the menu written on it across the desk top. "I've already put an order in at the local grocery store. They've assured me everything requested will arrive tomorrow."

"And she agrees people from the Big Apple are going to enjoy hickory smoked turkey with blueberry walnut stuffing?" Nikki sputtered looking up from the napkin with doubt filled eyes. "I can't imagine that they would think any of this would live up to what they are used to at weddings of this caliber."

"I understand your concerns. However, as I pointed out to Kenna, they aren't in New York City. They are here in the mountains surrounded by snow where it's relaxing and a bit romantic as well," Seth suggested wanting to assure her that he had things well in hand. He wanted to move off the subject of the menu he'd used to be able to talk to her. He knew she'd be hesitant to talk about what had happened in the lobby earlier.

"What better way to showcase the inn than with an elegant yet homey meal that will warm their hearts and souls?" Seth coaxed playing to her emotions on what the inn was meant to be seen as.

"It's your call, Chef. As long as you and the wedding planner have agreed and you've already ordered what you need, then who am I to say otherwise," Nikki declared pointedly. "If that's all, I have to figure out where to put our unexpected guest."

"I didn't know Payton was the photographer. If I had I never would have signed the contract," Seth explained. "Which means that we wouldn't have reconnected."

"Is that what you think we've done, *reconnected?*" Nikki choked.

"Not in that way, Nikki; at least not right away," Seth assured her even though he himself wanted more. More than he may have a right to even hope for. He did know he wanted nothing more than to find out if Nikki might still harbor that spark of love she once had for him. The love that he knew was still deep inside kept him from being involved with anyone over the last twenty-five years.

"But I'd like to think that we might have started to become friends again. If it eventually leads to more, I'm willing to find out," he said holding close the hope she felt the same way.

"Seth," Nikki groaned tears filling her eyes. "I don't know if I can give you what you think you want. I'll admit that old feelings were starting to surface, but after seeing the way Payton was looking at you—"

"I don't love her, Nikki. I don't want her in my life. She's not the woman for me. In fact she never was," Seth objected, tapping down his temper.

"It's obvious to me that she doesn't feel the same way, Seth," Nikki observed. "I believe she found out you were here and thought it would be a great opportunity for a reconciliation."

"This is the way she has always been. You don't know her like I do," Seth said pleading his case. "She doesn't love me. I can't give her what she really wants. She's had a string of failed romances that left a trail of broken hearts."

"People can change, Seth," Nikki reasoned. "She was your wife. Don't pass up this second chance to make things right between the two of you.

"Now, I must continue looking over Kenna's instructions. I'll talk to you later," she said, dismissing him and turned back to the papers spread out on her desk.

"She's not the second chance that I want, Nikki," Seth muttered walking out the door only to glance back at the woman who'd always held his heart realizing he'd do anything to win her back.

CHAPTER NINE

A Few Days Later

Nikki stood looking out her office window. She'd been keeping to herself as the wedding preparations took over her inn. Other than her employees, she'd had a few conversations with Kenna Blackstone, the wedding planner and organizer, on placement of furniture to make room for decorations and invited guests.

As for Seth, well, she'd seen very little of him since their conversation regarding his ex-wife's unexpected arrival. Nikki found that she missed him more than she'd admit to anyone but herself.

She longed to have a quick meal with him and discuss anything and everything. Whenever she went into the kitchen to get a plate of food, he was far too busy to even notice she was there. It would be Gabby who assisted her.

Nikki understood, but still, feeling hurt surprised her. Made her feel odd inside as if something was missing. Only she knew exactly what that something was…Seth.

"I've got to get out of here and away from all this hustle and bustle," she murmured making up her mind to take a walk. She wrapped a long, knit scarf around her neck and slipped into her heavy wool coat.

"I'm going to go for a walk, Ashley. I won't be long," she said passing the lobby desk without giving her faithful desk clerk a chance to respond.

Stepping out the door, she took a deep breath filling her lungs with the fresh, crisp air and smiled. *Freedom,* she thought pulling lined gloves over her hands.

Turning toward the foothills, Nikki rolled things over and over in her mind trying to make sense of her feelings. The wind stung her cheeks as she turned the corner, but she welcomed it. For several minutes the cold wind chaffed her skin and she suddenly felt a chill down her spine. Not from the cold but from the sense of being watched.

"Beautiful weather, isn't it?" The question was meant to be sarcastic more than anything else.

Payton Sinclair. Nikki quickly put a smile on her face and the distaste she felt for the woman in check before turning around.

"I always find it refreshing to come out and clear my mind," Nikki answered, holding her ground. "Winter in the mountains is cold, beautiful, and dangerous at times."

"I prefer the warmth of the summers myself," Payton said, holding her camera in her hands. "But I will admit that there is a beauty here that would be lost in the city. An innocence I think."

"There are many things that could get lost no matter what they are," Nikki said glancing from Payton to the inn behind them. "Have you been able to get some good shots of the bride and groom these past few days? The weather has thankfully been cooperative since the last storm when you arrived."

"As a matter of fact, I have," Payton affirmed shrewdly. "Especially the gazebo. It's a quaint little area that I hope will give that romantic feeling when they see them. Of course, I can't take any pictures of them together after dinner tonight. Bad luck and all that wedding superstitious nonsense. The rest of the photo shoot will have to wait until tomorrow."

"You don't believe in fate either then I take it?" Nikki asked not at all surprised. Payton Sinclair didn't strike her as the kind of woman who waited for things to happen; she made them happen whether good or bad.

"No, I believe in being in control of my own destiny. Wishing and hoping are for silly, little girls," Payton said off handedly. "I've always gotten what I wanted my entire life, and I don't foresee that changing any time soon."

Nikki's suspicion grew. Payton Sinclair was up to something and she had a sinking feeling it had to do with either her or Seth—or both. If anything happened to ruin this wedding, it would more than likely destroy the reputation of the inn as well as herself.

"What do you believe in, Ms. Reed? Fairy tales and true love?" Payton sneered, a mocking grin on her ruby red lips.

"As a matter of fact I do. I also believe in poisonous apples and wicked queens," Nikki remarked. "I also believe in good things happening to good people. And in Santa of course."

When Payton squinted at her a sense of evil crept into Nikki's mind. This woman was exactly how Seth tried to describe her. Now Nikki understood why he couldn't find a place for her in his heart even after the forced marriage.

"Christmas Eve and the wedding is tomorrow. We never know what Santa will have in his bag for us all," Nikki said, smiling as she walked past the woman she realized was her rival not only in the past but the present also.

"Ms. Reed," Payton called out. "Don't think I don't know who you are because I do. You are the silly girl who has always been in Seth's heart. I hope you don't make the same mistake twice because if you do, be sure I'm here to pick up the pieces once again."

Nikki turned around and walked straight back to Payton.

"Don't worry, Miss Sinclair, I have no intention of taking what isn't mine," Nikki said calmly, then returned to the inn, every inch of her body shaking inside and out.

"WHAT IN THE devil is going on out there?" Seth muttered, lingering at the lobby window watching Nikki and Payton. "If she says or does anything to hurt Nikki, she'll live to regret it."

He grew nervous and helpless watching Payton continue to approach Nikki. He sensed the tension in Nikki and admired the way she looked to be holding her own. Payton was a master at spinning a web of deceit around an unsuspecting person. Especially someone like Nikki who may never have met a person as mean spirited as his ex-wife.

"Seth, here you are. I haven't had a chance to tell you how sorry I am about Payton," Kenna apologized as she stood beside him. "She called immediately after I got the news from the Drakes. I had no choice but to offer her the job on such short notice."

"Did she know I was under contract?" Seth asked, holding his breath.

"If she did, I have no knowledge of how she found out," Kenna replied. "You care for her, don't you?"

"Are you crazy? I haven't cared for Payton in over twenty-five years," Seth spat.

"I was referring to Ms. Reed, not Payton," Kenna said softly. "I've seen the way you two are together. There's something brewing between the two of you, isn't there?"

"Once, long ago there was," Seth mused. "I'd hoped that maybe there could be again when I saw her the other day. I had no idea she owned this inn. I never knew what happened to her after…"

"Don't give up hope. There's always magic at Christmas," Kenna said patting his shoulder as she walked away leaving him to his observations.

"I hope there's some magic left for us," he replied under his breath noticing Nikki walk away from Payton.

Drawing in a breath, he sat down in a chair near the door and waited. He was going to set the record straight either way regardless of which one of them walked through the door first.

"How people can live in this part of the country is beyond me," Payton complained, shedding her coat.

"Then why did you manipulate your way here?" Seth asked crossing his arms across his chest.

"Because of you of course, and you know that," Payton cooed, strolling through the entry way over to where he now stood.

"You already have my answer where that is concerned, Payton. It hasn't changed since the other day," he reminded her.

"And what of your *Mrs.* Reed? Has your opinion of the one that got away changed?" she asked a smirk on her face.

"You know who she is?" His heart fell to the pit of his stomach as he fought to control his surprise. "Or have you known all these years?"

"Would I be here otherwise? I think not," Payton huffed. "Your happiness, rather lack of, is my life's work. You ruined my plans by leaving your father's firm, so why shouldn't I do you the same service?"

"It really bothers you so much that for at least once in your life, you didn't get exactly what you wanted?" Seth asked even though he knew the answer. Payton didn't like losing to anyone on anything.

"Oh, I'm working on a remedy for that." She laughed than continued on her way.

Seth shook his head, his gaze following Payton's retreat. When he turned around Nikki stood in the doorway.

NIKKI WAITED JUST inside the door trying to absorb every word she heard. Payton knew who she was before coming here and it sounded like she'd known for years. Nikki wondered if the so-called emergency the other photographer had was fabricated or not.

What did it matter? The woman planned on being a thorn in Seth's side and Nikki felt sorry for him.

"Nikki."

"Not now, Seth," she said pulling off her gloves and

shoving them into her coat pocket. "I have last minute things to do. Besides, don't you have food to prepare for the wedding tomorrow?"

"Everything that can be done ahead of time is complete," Seth remarked advancing toward her.

"Good," she said heading toward her office. "As I said, I have work to do."

"So you say," Seth replied following so close behind her she could feel him. "I can talk while you work."

"Suit yourself, but really Seth," Nikki said hanging up her coat then settling in behind her desk. "There isn't anything to talk about, not really. And especially not now."

"Of course there is and you know it," Seth countered sitting on the arm of the chair across from her. "I saw you outside. What did Payton say to you?"

"Nothing of any importance," she said pretending to look at the page in front of her. How was she going to tell him what she really thought of his former wife?

"So she was civil and polite as usual then. That's good," Seth surmised, nodding his head.

"If you call having to face a cobra polite and civil, then yes," Nikki said, sitting back in her chair. "She's very bitter, I'm afraid. And, for whatever reason, has felt she needed to get into my business and find out all she could about me even from thirty years ago."

"I bet my father had something to do with that," Seth muttered shaking his head. "Thankfully that is all over with."

"A woman scorned is a woman to beware of," she warned, chewing her bottom lip. "She knew you were here. She knew I owned the inn long before you did."

"Maybe now you understand why there's no chance of a reconciliation with her," Seth said kneeling down next to her. "You are the only woman to ever have my heart, Nikki. The only one I've thought about all these years. The one I long to spend to rest of my life with. Don't you see that?"

"I need time to think about it Seth. When the wedding is over you'll go back to your life far from the one I lead here," she said sadness creeping into her usually well controlled emotions. "I'm not sure I could give all of this up, not even for love."

"Twenty-four hours. I'll have your answer then," Seth agreed as Ashley came in with an envelope in her hand. "But I'm not going to give up that easily when it comes to not letting you go this time. I made that mistake once. I'll not make it again."

"Did you need something, Ashley?" Nikki asked as Seth slipped by a wide-eyed young lady.

"Oh, yes. This came for you from town," Ashley said handing over the envelope.

"Thank you. Now go eat and take the rest of the day off. Put up the sign directing people to my office if they need assistance. Tomorrow is a big day around here and I want you and everyone else well rested," Nikki smiled, slicing the envelope open as the desk clerk padded out of her office.

Slipping the telegram from inside, she read the message and leaned back in her chair. As if she needed any more bad vibes, now Chef Winston had decided to retire.

CHAPTER TEN

Christmas Eve

"I hope everyone is ready for this event," Seth said looking over his sleepy-eyed staff. "Most of the dishes have been prepared ahead of time; now it is only a matter of making sure the food is hot. This morning we'll prepare the remaining items.

"Gabby, you'll oversee the Waldorf salad, squash margarita puff, hot rolls, and champagne making sure all are all prepared to perfection and ready to plate as soon as the ceremony is over.

"Anyone else that hasn't been assigned a task, I'm counting on you to make the dining room feel as warm and inviting as ever before. All the chafing dishes will need to be warm and kept filled. Any questions?"

"No, Chef!"

"Good, let's get to work then," he said clapping his hands. "Gabby, I'd like to have a word with you when you have a free moment."

"Yes, Chef. After the reception?" Gabby asked.

"Perfect," Seth answered then slipped out of the kitchen. He'd already made the decision last night to offer her a position as head chef at his New York restaurant. He had complete faith in her skills and hated seeing them being waste at the inn.

If Gabby accepted, he'd find a suitable sous-chef replacement for Chef Winston. Seth wouldn't leave neither Nikki nor Winston in the lurch without a good sous-chef.

"Everything looks great in here Seth," Kenna said from the dining room entrance. "In fact, everything about the inn is so refreshing. I've spoken with the bride and groom and they are more than pleased with the decision to have their wedding here. In fact, they plan on celebrating their anniversary every year at the inn."

"Ms. Reed will be pleased to know that," Seth said, proud for what Nikki had accomplished with the inn, giving him all the more reason to move on with his life.

"Oh, and I've already told her this morning. She's in her office finalizing paperwork if you're interested." Kenna winked then walked away.

Seth wanted more than anything to go to Nikki and share in her victory but would wait until he'd had a chance to talk with Gabby. If he was going to tell Nikki of his decision to stay and not go back to New York City he had to have the plan in place first.

"Seth?" Payton's voice pierced his thoughts.

No, not today of all days!

"What is it, Payton? If you're here to try to convince me to take you back after all these years don't even try," Seth reiterated, turning back toward the kitchen.

"Well that thought has crossed my mind as you well know, but for now I need your help," Payton said standing there looking all sweet and innocent which should have been his first warning.

"With what?" Seth asked lifting an eyebrow.

"I'd like to take some pictures of the happy couple to be in the kitchen, if that works for you," Payton said tossing her long hair over a shoulder.

"As a matter of fact, it doesn't. The staff is very busy and having the extra people getting in the way will only hinder things," Seth said. "What about using the dining room and they can act like they are doing whatever it is you want them to be doing?"

"As long as you will be there to oversee in case I need something from the kitchen," Payton said crossing the room, her camera grasped in her hands.

"Anything to get you off my back for the rest of the day," Seth agreed.

"Thank you so much, Seth," Payton said, leaning to kiss him.

"Stop it!" Seth hissed moving away before her lips landed on his. "You aren't ever going to learn, are you?"

Shaking his head, Seth walked back to the kitchen which was as far from her as he could get at the moment given the circumstances.

NIKKI SWIPED at the tear trailing down her cheek. Seeing Payton give Seth a kiss was all the proof she needed to know that Payton still cared for Seth. There was no room in his life for her. And to think she was going to tell him about Miles retiring and ask Seth to stay on at the inn at least until she could find a suitable permanent replacement.

Sliding in behind her desk, she picked up the phone and dialed Miles's number. If she had to get down on her knees and beg him to stay she would.

"Hello," a sweet lady's voice echoed in her ear.

"Hi, I'm calling for Miles Winston. Is he available?" Nikki asked surprised that a woman had answered the phone.

"One moment please," the woman said. "Miles, it's for you."

"Miles here," Miles said his voice a comfort to Nikki's senses.

"Hi, Miles," Nikki said softly afraid she'd start reciting all the reasons she needed him to stay.

"Ms. Reed, what can I do for you?"

"I got your telegram. Are you sure you want to retire?" Nikki asked hoping it was only a ploy to get her sympathy for having to leave when Seth arrived.

"Yes. Coming home made me realize how much I missed family. And it is time for me to hang up my apron and hand it over to a younger chef with new ideas," Miles said with a relaxed and happy tone Nikki hadn't heard before.

"Miles, how am I going to replace the genius behind the brand of Gingerbread Inn?" Nikki asked tears welling up in her eyes.

"Gabby knows all my recipes. I'll send a legal document giving you permission to use them at the inn," Miles offered.

"Your offer is very generous and I thank you for all the years you've given me," Nikki said.

"Merry Christmas, Nikki," Miles said then broke the connection.

"Merry Christmas, Miles," she whispered putting the phone down.

"Now what am I going to do?" she muttered sinking her head deep into her hands. "At least I have a few months to find a replacement. It shouldn't be that hard to find someone?"

"Trouble in paradise, Ms. Reed," Payton snickered.

"No, not at all. What can I do for you, Miss Sinclair?" Nikki asked hoping the woman would be the first to leave in the morning.

"Kenna sent me to tell you that the wedding will be starting in about five minutes." Payton clucked. "I'm not sure why it should matter to you, but there you have it. Your invitation."

"Thank you, Payton," Nikki said checking her watch. What she had to do would have to wait until after the wedding.

"Yes, well then I have a wedding to photograph," Payton said turning on her heel and stomping out of Nikki's office.

"One more day, just one more day and I can relax," Nikki said, making her way out to the lobby where two young people's lives were about to change.

SETH STOOD on the outskirts of the dining room, watching as the newly married couple smashed cake into each other's faces. He was pleased with the way Gabby had taking the reins and prepared the dining room. The guests would have plenty to eat and drink to their fill.

"Chef, is now a good time?" Gabby asked standing next to him. "I can spare a few minutes."

"Of course. I'll meet you in a minute," Seth said scanning the room quickly. He hadn't seen Nikki since the vows were said.

Walking into the kitchen he was surprised to find Nikki and Gabby chatting. Nikki glanced over at him and he thought she looked a bit frazzled.

"Thank about it, Gabby, and let me know after Christmas."

Seth overheard Nikki say before she hurried out of the kitchen on the opposite side.

"What's going on, Gabby?" he asked, worried that something must have happened.

"Chef Winston is retiring and Ms. Reed asked me to take over until she can find a qualified replacement," Gabby said, her eyes wide in astonishment.

"Retired? Chef Winston?" Seth gasped. "Do what you feel is best, Gabby. I'm sorry but I've got to find Nikki, er, Ms. Reed."

Seth hurried through the kitchen and through the inn looking for Nikki. Finding her office empty save for her winter coat, he had a feeling where he would find her. The one place no one would bother to go...the shed.

Half walking half running through the lobby, Seth pushed open the door, the cold wind hitting him squarely in the face. His eyes blurred and he blinked twice to clear them. Wrapping his arms around himself, he ran over to the slightly ajar door and slid inside closing it behind him.

"Nikki?" he called walking slowly over to the tractor where he found her huddled inside the cab. "Are you okay?"

"No, not really," she answered sniffing. "Everything is slowly falling apart and I don't seem to be able to stop it."

"Has Payton done something?" Seth asked, sliding in next to her, having an idea Payton Sinclair had nothing to do with Nikki's distress.

"Not this time." Nikki laughed swiping away tears with a gloved hand. "Chef Winston is retiring and the only good thing is that he's going to let me have his gingerbread recipes. He said that Gabby was able to cover until I find a replacement."

"For once I agree with him about Gabby. She's wasting her talent here, Nikki," Seth said, taking her hands in his. "I have a solution to your chef problem, at least for a while."

"You know of someone then?" Nikki asked her eyes lighting up for a brief moment.

"Yes," Seth said rubbing the top of her gloved hand with his thumb. "I wasn't going to say anything until I knew for sure. I wanted to wait until everyone was gone, but I see I can't wait.

"I was going to offer Gabby the head chef position at my restaurant. I decided last night that I no longer belong in New York."

"You what!?" Nikki exclaimed pulling her hands out of his. "You were going to poach one of my cooks?"

"Gabby needs to spread her wings and fly. She deserves the right to experience things she'll never experience here," Seth said, sitting on his hands to keep from pulling her close to him.

"And what about you? If you don't return to New York City, what are your plans?" Nikki asked questions glowing in her eyes.

"I belong here, with you Nikki," Seth said softly, his body slumped forward.

"What about Payton?"

"There's only one person I want to have a second chanced with and that's you," Seth confessed taking her into his arms. "If you'll have me that is. I hope with all my being that you will."

"I didn't realize until I saw you with Payton in the dining room how much I wanted a second chance as well," Nikki said.

Seth pulled her closer, gently kissing her lips. He was home where he belonged and he'd never let anyone tell him any different.

EPILOGUE

Christmas Day

ikki and Seth stood next to each other saying goodbye to the wedding party.

Kenna Blackstone had already booked a summer wedding for the next year. The newly married Mr. and Mrs. Hathaway made their reservations to return on their one-year anniversary.

Gabby had accepted Seth's offer of a head chef position in his restaurant after the first of year. Seth would be traveling back to New York with her only to introduce her to the kitchen staff and to make sure her first week went smoothly. He reassured her he was only a phone call away if she needed him.

Payton stopped in front of them, pulling her bag behind her with a bit of defeat. "I don't know if I really believe this is happening to me again. But I hope you are both happy."

Nikki stepped forward, giving Payton a hug. "You'll find the one, Payton," she whispered before stepping back to Seth's side allowing Payton to huff her way out the door.

"Are you happy, Seth?" Nikki asked concern echoing on her words.

"Not fully," he said wrapping his arms around her.

"No, why not?" Nikki asked, looking up into his face.

"I will be once you agree to be my wife, Nikki Reed," he said getting down on one knee.

"As if you had to ask," Nikki declared tears streaming down her face. As she took his hands in hers she felt the swirl of Christmas magic.

THE END

Thank you for reading *Gingerbread Inn (Christmas at the Inn, Book 13)* I hope you will read the next in the series, *Snowflake Inn* on November, 25, 2022.

When a merry matchmaker brings two lonely people together, will a Christmas love follow?

Gina Snow's life imploded after her fiancé dumped her and stole her dream job as a pastry chef at a famous hotel. Now she's come back to temporarily run her uncle Dan's Snowflake Inn after he had a series of mini strokes. She'll keep the inn going while he finishes rehab. Then maybe she'll try to get a life. One thing she knows is romance is not in the cards for her. She vows never to mix love and business again

Jessie Barnes, a wounded ex-warrior recently dismissed from the same rehab facility, is hungry to complete one more mission. He's come to the inn, taking Dan up on his request that he manage the inn so Gina is not burdened and can follow her dreams.

Can Gina and Jessie work together? Will they find the piece of their heart that each is missing when they come together? To find out, take a trip with me to the *Snowflake Inn.*

ABOUT THE AUTHOR

Maxine Douglas first began writing in the early 1970s while in high school. She took every creative writing course offered at the time and focused her energy for many years after that on poetry. It wasn't until a dear friend's sister revealed she was about to become a published author that jumpstarted Maxine into getting the ball rolling; she finished her first manuscript in a month's time.

Maxine Douglas and her late husband moved to Oklahoma in 2010 from Wisconsin. Since then Maxine has rekindled her childhood love of westerns. She has four children, two granddaughters, and a German Shorthair Pointer named Missy. And many friends she now considers her Oklahoma family.

One of the things Maxine has learned over the years is that you can never stop dreaming and reaching for the stars. Sooner or later you touch one and it'll bring you more happiness than you can ever imagine. Maxine feels lucky, and blessed, that over the past several years she's been able to reach out and touch the stars--and she's still reaching.

Maxine loves to hear from her readers. So, come on by and say "Hello"; Maxine would love to hear from you. You can catch her on:

Facebook Reader Group: https://www.facebook.com/groups/maxinesbookdivas/
Twitter: @waMaxineDouglas
Blog: http://maxinedouglasauthor.blogspot.com/
Goodreads: https://www.goodreads.com/author/show/6423715.Maxine_Douglas
BookBub: https://www.bookbub.com/authors/maxine-douglas

www.ingramcontent.com/pod-product-compliance
Lightning Source LLC
Chambersburg PA
CBHW051856130726

47987CB00002B/865